T0165681

GOODNIGHT, ROSE

CHI ZIJIAN

Translated from the Chinese by
POPPY TOLAND

VIKING
an imprint of
PENGUIN BOOKS

VIKING

UK | USA | Canada | Ireland | Australia
India | New Zealand | South Africa | China

Penguin Books is part of the Penguin Random House group of companies
whose addresses can be found at global.penguinrandomhouse.com.

Penguin
Random House
PENGUIN BOOKS

This hardback edition is published by Penguin Group (Australia) in association with
Penguin (Beijing) Ltd, 2018

1 3 5 7 9 10 8 6 4 2

Text copyright © Chi Zijian, 2018
Translation copyright © Poppy Toland, 2018

Translated from the Chinese by Poppy Toland
Originally published in Chinese as *Wan'an Meigui* by People's
Literature Publishing House

Cover design by Di Suo © Penguin Random House (Australia)
Text design by Steffan Leyshon-Jones © Penguin Group (Australia)
Printed and bound in China by RR Donnelley

A catalogue record for this book is available from the National Library of Australia.

ISBN: 9780734399106

penguin.com.au

GOODNIGHT, ROSE

I

Ji Lianna was my third Harbin landlord and in her eighties when we first met.

She lived in Daoli district, near Central Avenue. Her house was in a three-storey building made from brick and wood, constructed seventy or eighty years before in the style of a Russian garden villa. It had a delightful pointy roof, an open balcony, tall narrow windows and gently sloping steps. The building stood out against its pale grey concrete jungle surroundings. It was like a fawn tiptoeing up to the edge of a lake to drink: young and clumsy, charming and playful. A café occupied the ground floor of the building, while the first and second floors provided residential housing for six families. Ji Lianna lived in a southwest-facing apartment on the second floor. The two bedrooms and the living room were all very spacious, while the kitchen, bathroom and balcony were small but well structured, and the high ceilings meant that the place never felt cramped. Ji Lianna's apartment was nice and light, dotted with vibrant plants and flowers that made the space beautiful and full of life – unlike her face, which was as cold and gloomy as the northern midwinter wilderness. She was tall, slim and never hunched her shoulders, which meant that from behind, you could easily mistake her for a young girl. That was only when she was standing still, of course. As soon as she started to walk her footsteps would expose her age as they fell slow, heavy and laborious.

It was Huang Weina, a journalist from the news department at the local newspaper where I worked, who suggested I rent a room at Ji Lianna's. She met her while working on an article about people of Jewish descent living in Harbin. Ji Lianna had never married and she lived on her own. Her parents had died long ago, and she had no other relatives. Despite her advanced years, she coped well, and didn't even employ a cleaner, but Huang Weina sensed that she was lonely and vulnerable. 'Such a splendid house, why not rent out a room?' Huang Weina asked. 'Wouldn't you enjoy having someone around to talk to?' Ji Lianna explained that she never felt lonely because *He* was always there. It was at that moment I happened to call Huang Weina to tell her I'd moved out from my second lodgings and that all my suitcases were piled up at my work's reception. I had nowhere to go, and begged her to help me find somewhere else to live as soon as possible.

Huang Weina knew about my fallout with my first landlord, a scrawny retiree who accosted me in an attempt to get his wicked way. He'd come to see me when his wife was out playing mahjong one evening, naked from the waist down, with a wad of greasy banknotes in his hand. He'd pushed open the door to my room and grabbed me, saying he'd halve my rent if I obliged him, and give me some extra spending money as well. I struggled against him, knocking the money from his hand and scratching his face. The money was all in notes of twos and fives – he must have been saving it up for some time. He begged me not to be put off by how old and thin he was; he was still as adept as ever beneath the sheets, it was just his wife hadn't let him anywhere near since her menopause. Going to prostitutes was too risky, so he just suffered in miserable silence. His tears mixed with the blood seeped from the scratch forming a revolting mess on his face, which looked like a miniature abattoir. I wrenched myself free and ran down the stairs. I crouched next to the rubbish bin and vomited, and then with my hands trembling, I dialled Huang Weina's number. I moved out that same night. Huang Weina urged me to report him to the police, but I refused. It wasn't out of pity for the old man, but because I was a plain girl who'd never attracted the attention of the right kind of man. I worried that if news of this police investigation got out, I might be viewed as a rape victim, a dirty rag, which would make it even harder for me to meet someone decent.

Huang Weina worked as a journalist, and with her extensive network of contacts, including a large number of agency bosses, she managed to find me new lodgings in no time. My next landlady was a 28-year-old congenitally deaf girl called Liu Qin, a name simple enough for herself to pronounce. Liu Qin's parents and brother were all deaf, too. They were a family of Chinese medical specialists who ran a successful acupuncture and physical therapy clinic on the bank of the Songhua River. Having made some money, they bought a spacious house in Xinyang Road where the family lived their silent but fulfilled lives. Liu Qin had been scared of needles since she was young and couldn't stand seeing patients with all those spikes sticking out of them. Aged nineteen, she found herself a job washing dishes in the canteen of a primary school near Jiaohua Square in Nangang district, but found the commute through two districts to get there a frustrating waste of time. Eventually, she decided it would be better to rent somewhere near the school. Aware that their daughter would probably get married soon, Liu Qin's parents decided to buy her an apartment where she could live instead of renting. Their bank savings had devalued in recent years, while housing prices only went up, so property seemed like a smart investment. They bought a two-bedroom apartment below the Anfa Flyover in Nangang, a fifteen-minute walk from the school where she worked. Liu Qin's mother worried about her daughter living all alone and regularly went over to keep her company. After Liu Qin's brother married and his wife had a baby, Liu Qin's mother found herself otherwise engaged and decided to find a nice lodger for her daughter's place instead. Huang Weina met the family when writing a piece about their clinic and knew they were on the lookout for a lodger. So the day after I left my first landlord, I had a new place to stay. Liu Qin only charged me 600 *yuan* a month, including water, gas and electricity, while my old landlord had charged me 700, excluding water and electricity and hadn't allowed me to use the gas.

Huang Weina had just finished interviewing Ji Lianna and they were both sitting in the café below her apartment when I called. 'You're not going to tell me that she acted indecently towards you as well? I know that lesbianism was all the rage these days, but really!' she joked when I told her I was moving out from Liu Qin's. 'But didn't you and Liu Qin get on well?' she asked, serious now. 'What went wrong? You know you're not going to find another Harbin landlord half as good.' 'She's getting married!' I croaked. 'I can't live there anymore.'

'So it wasn't your choice to move out then,' she said kindly. She comforted me; saying I should not worry. My perfect landlord was just around the corner. She would come straight over to pick me up and take me back to hers where I could stay for a couple days.

When Huang Weina had finished speaking with me, she turned to Ji Lianna and said, 'Well there's a coincidence! Only moments after suggesting you get a lodger, I find out my good friend has just become homeless!'

Ji Lianna frowned and looked serious for a while, before commencing on a careful line of questioning about my situation, such as where did my family live, how old was I, did I have a boyfriend or a penchant for eating pork, did I regularly change my clothes and wash my shirts, did I snore, suffer from hay fever, like listening to the piano, was I an introvert or an extrovert, was I in the habit of losing keys – all of which Huang Weina answered. Ji Lianna thought about it then said, 'Why don't you invite her here so I can meet her?'

Huang Weina called me straight back to tell me that she had a house that could be the answer to my prayers, and I should go round there as soon as possible. She excused herself to go to the bathroom and while she was there, sent me a text message saying: *When you come here in a bit to meet her, remember to act slightly more demure than usual! If she does ask you to live at hers, you'll experience Harbin from a hundred years ago in all its classic elegance! I expect she'll only ask for token rent. You've really landed on your feet - Hooray!* she added in Russian.

It was late autumn, and as I opened the door to the café, a gust of wind blew past me shaking the last few dried leaves from the elm tree by the door. They tumbled from the branches and two of them landed right on my head. Huang Weina told me they were lucky leaves and they brightened up my appearance, making it look as if I was wearing two gold clips in my hair.

The first time I saw Ji Lianna, I felt slightly overawed. She had fair skin, and wore a grey-green woollen dress and had a heavy black silk scarf with a light silver-grey pattern around her neck. Her large grey-blue eyes shone, but carried a sense of gloom, and her Roman nose cast a charming shadow over her face. Her attire was elegant, while my clothes were vulgar. I had tear-stained cheeks and my hair was all over the place. I was wearing a red flowery jumper and brown trousers because I'd been in a hurry to move out of Liu Qin's, and purple plimsolls on my feet, which, Huang Weina told me, made me look like a garish flamingo.

Timidly I took hold of Ji Lianna's outstretched hand, and in a trembling voice I said, 'My name is Zhao Xiao'e.' At that moment, I remembered the mother who'd named me, recalled how we'd lowered her into the ground, and my tears started to flow.

Seeing that I had lost my composure, Huang Weina hurriedly tried to think of an excuse. 'Both our names have *Na* in them, and hers doesn't, and it's made her so jealous she's burst into tears,' she said to Ji Lianna.

'Is the *e* in your name the same as in Chang'e the moon Goddess?' Ji Lianna asked gently.

I wiped my eyes and nodded.

Ji Lianna dropped her head, muttering, 'All three of us have names with Chinese characters that carry the woman radical. *He* must have arranged this.' She turned to me and said, 'If you want to be a strong girl you shouldn't cry in front of others, Xiao'e. And if you still want the room you are welcome to move in with me in three days' time. I won't ask you for any rent, just 200 *yuan* per month for water, gas and electricity. I can't promise that this will be a long-term arrangement, but let's just see how it goes.' Having said this, Ji Lianna returned to her seat, and continued to drink her coffee.

Huang Weina and I looked at each other, unable to believe my luck. We thanked Ji Lianna and left the café. As soon as we turned the corner, Huang Weina, no longer able to control her excitement, hugged me right there in the street.

'I've only ever dreamed of living in a house like that,' she gushed. 'You really are so lucky! Whenever you leave one house, a better one comes along! I must warn you, she's not keen on living with a girl who has a boyfriend. So when she asks you about that, just give a little white lie. Remember, whatever you do, don't take your boyfriend back to her house – you'll have plenty of places you can meet him: the park, restaurants, tea houses, the cinema, his room; and if it's not convenient for you two to have personal time there, you can always get a room at a motel – it won't cost much.'

'There'll be no need for that. I'm single again.'

'What! Dumped again?' Huang Weina said, stamping her feet. 'By him – that dwarf who guzzled food like a pig, grunting away? How can a minor civil servant without a house or a car dare to be that picky!'

2

The same evening as I moved into Ji Lianna's, I was admiring the potted plants in the living room when she suddenly started walking over to me with a pair of scissors. It wasn't right for young girls to perm their hair, she explained to me. If one didn't keep a head full of fleece-like curls well-tended, it started to look like a hay bale – horribly messy – and her advice for me was to cut it all off. I'd been planning to get rid of this clump of weeds, even if she hadn't said anything. Song Xiangkui had been the one who'd convinced me to perm my hair in the first place. I had a narrow forehead, and my face was too thin, making me look like a famine victim, according to him, and perming my hair would remedy this facial *defect* and make me look more feminine. *A girl will go to any length to look good for the man she loves*. I'd heard this sentiment being spoken a lot, so I let him take me to the beauty parlour, where I endured two hours of what felt like torture that left me looking like a Pekinese terrier. Huang Weina thought I looked hideous with my perm, and I became the source of constant ridicule; her most amusing quip being that I looked like Beethoven reincarnated. I'd never actually liked the curls, and now that Song Xiangkui had left me, cutting them off felt like severing myself from my old life. So, why not?

Ji Lianna sat me down on a hard wooden chair, covered my neck with a grey towel and started to cut my hair. Snip, snip, snip, went the scissors, defeating the enemy. The scissors seemed very sharp, and she seemed extremely skilled. It took her all of about ten minutes to finish cutting my hair. Ji Lianna looked me over carefully, nodded and then guided me over to the bathroom mirror.

Where had I gone? Was that girl really me? The person in front of me had short, fine, boyish hair, slightly fluffy on top, with subtle waves, and a jagged fringe over my forehead covering my *defect*. My small eyes seemed to have grown larger and my nose didn't look as sunken. I looked about ten years younger, my face shining with an uncanny cuteness. 'Oh, it appears I'm not as ugly as I thought,' I said. 'Hair is a girl's motorbike,' explained Ji Lianna. 'If you work it well, you can make yourself beautiful!' 'Thank you so much, granny!' I blurted in my over-excited state. Ji Lianna's face fell. Wiping her scissors with a damp flannel, she said, 'You will call me Ji Lianna.' It was only later having regained my composure that I realised a woman who had never married had probably retained her young girl's spirit, and even though she was my grandmother's age, it was inappropriate to call her granny.

I'd never met a woman quite so keen on gardening. Ji Lianna's horticulture created the perfect marriage between aesthetics and practicality. She essentially grew all the vegetables she ate. The long wooden trough under the balcony window looked as if it was simply blooming with English marigolds, while actually there were burnet roots growing amongst the flowers. At first glance at the three big clay flowerpots on the living room balcony, you were greeted with fire-red hydrangea, light-yellow michelia and a colourful array of pansies. Looking more closely, however, you would notice growing among the hydrangeas the slender stems of spring onions, and mint leaves nestling up among the michelia, while brightly coloured chilli peppers gave the pansies a run for their money. Spider plants kept company with chives on the bookshelves, while glossy green patchouli crept underneath the calla lilies in the bedroom. Ji Lianna only ate two meals a day, and opposite to most people, her evening meal consisted of milk, mutton sausage, fried egg and salad, while for breakfast she ate either beef or fish soup with bread. She liked to sprinkle her salads and soups with her homegrown herbs. And the salads she made always had a hint of burnet root. Every afternoon, Ji Lianna would go down to the café downstairs to drink coffee, and after that she would go to Central Avenue to buy two bread buns from Modern – she never ate yesterday's bread. Once a week she'd make a trip to the Xiulong Street market where she'd buy enough food for the week. As a member of the Jewish faith she didn't eat pork, a restriction she took very seriously, and I never brought pork into the house, even though I adored sweet-and-sour pork ribs. We were similar in that we both loved fruit, apples and pineapple in particular, and so sometimes I'd buy extra, so I had some to give her.

I worked at the newspaper office as a proofreader. If you looked at the newspaper as a series of fields, I was the one who did the weeding. It was my job to pluck out all the incorrect characters and faulty sentences. During my days off, I enjoyed a lie-in. Often when I woke up and came to, I'd start to smell the lovely aromas wafting out of the kitchen. When Ji Lianna saw I was up, she'd ask me if I'd like to eat a little something with her. Each time I'd fib about how I had plans to meet a friend, and after a quick wash, I'd go to the little restaurant outside to have a bowl of pork fried noodles with sesame paste, or some wontons. As I ate this, I'd always be thinking about Ji Lianna's dining table, the blue-flowered porcelain bowl with its golden rim filled with a thick soup being stirred by a shiny silver spoon. Her lifestyle was so utterly refined.

After Ji Lianna had transformed my hair, she started to makeover the way I dressed. She explained, that contrary to what I might think, wearing bright garish colours didn't make me look full of life, and actually it was plain, neutral colours that would bring out my sense of youthful energy. To prove this, she took a light-grey woollen shawl and styled it into a simple but attractive cape-style coat. When I started wearing it out, people at the office asked me what label it was, and told me it had a lovely cosmopolitan feel. Next, Ji Lianna instructed me to lay out all my clothes and told me which jacket should go with which trousers, and which shirt with which skirt. I didn't have many clothes, but after receiving her guidance on how to wear them, I felt as if my wardrobe had been enriched.

Ji Lianna had a rattan box inlaid with a Star of David where she kept her Hebrew Bible. She prayed three times a day, morning, noon and evening, during which she recited from the Bible in a quiet voice. Because I didn't understand Hebrew, it was like listening to gibberish each day. Another one of her habits was to sit at the piano in the living room fireplace as evening was drawing in, and play a few pieces. She kept a small square table next to the piano, which I always imagined as a musical note flying out of the piano. I constantly wondered to myself how a woman like Ji Lianna, with such a rich inner world, had never come to find love. I'd often look at the photographs arranged over the fireplace, and apart from those of family members, all the photos were of her on her own at different ages. From a young age right up until now, she'd always been a beauty.

Ji Lianna enjoyed silence and didn't speak much; nor did she sleep well. I always made sure that my bedroom door was shut tight at night, in case deep in the night when all was quiet I happened to emit a peaceful snore, and end up disturbing her. The living room contained a silent German wall clock, which I assumed was broken, however, when I asked her that one day she shook her head and said that it was a very well-made clock, but as she had gotten older she'd started to find its *tick-tock* sound unbearable, and had decided to stop it. Gazing at me earnestly she said, 'I don't dare start it up again. Imagine all these years it's been stopped – it must contain a bellyful of suppressed time. What if it's become brain-dead and decides to release all that saved up ticking at once, it would simply deafen me.' I thought that she was being humorous, but when I looked at her face, her expression was calm and sincere, far from that of one telling a joke. At certain times she seemed to be living in a fairytale world.

It wasn't long before a conflict developed between the two of us. I'd been washing my underwear one day, and seeing that the sun was shining, decided to hang it out on the balcony to dry. When Ji Lianna saw it there, she scolded me and ordered for me to take it down. She told me what

I'd done had been very bad-mannered. The balcony was for plants, and the clothes rack there was only supposed to hang tablecloths, sheets and outer garments. A gynaecologist had told me that ladies' underwear was best dried under the sun, as the sun had antibacterial qualities, and this made it healthier, I explained. 'Well you can go and use someone else's balcony in that case!' Lianna said, pointing to the door.

Following her orders, I begrudgingly took down my wet undergarments and stuffed them into a plastic bag, which I put inside my suitcase. I cried as I packed my suitcase, unable to believe my bad luck. I had no relatives in this city, no one who loved me, no money, and now not even a place to live – I was no better than a stray cat! If my landlady really was throwing me out, I had no idea whose eaves I'd wake up sheltering under tomorrow. Seeing that I really was planning to leave, Ji Lianna gave a sigh. She took out a handkerchief and helped me dry my tears, then she lifted the bag with my wet undergarments out of my suitcase and hung them back out on the balcony. Without giving any explanation, she pulled me down the stairs, her knee joints cracking so much they sounded as if there were axes hidden inside them, chopping at her legs as if against firewood. Once we were downstairs, she led me to the other side of the street, and pointed up at her balcony.

Sure enough, the undergarments hanging there did give off an air of indecency about them, a whiff of prostitution. I admitted my mistake right away, telling her I had been born in a small village in Keshan, and since I was small we'd washed our clothes at home and hung them all up together on the washing line in the yard, not even considering whether they were under or outer garments. Ji Lianna stroked my head sympathetically and said, 'In the city, the rooms inside your house are yours alone, but the balconies are not – you have to consider the eyes of passersby.'

In Harbin the beginning of winter was always the worst time. As soon as the government-provided central heating kicked in, all the city's chimneys came to life, puffing and belching out soot and smoke. If the air pressure happened to be low, the dust couldn't disperse, and the city would be so depressingly smoggy it would look as if it were wearing a lapis-coloured hat. On days like this, Ji Lianna's chronic bronchitis would flare up, and she'd be coughing morning to night. If she happened to be tending to her plants and flowers in the living room when she had one of these coughing fits, I'd assist by rubbing her back and fetching her a glass of water. Ji Lianna's shoulders would tremble and her face would turn slightly grey and I'd worry she might stop breathing and choke. She rarely ever spoke, but as soon as she started coughing, she'd begin lamenting in between the coughs. 'Harbin skies never used to be like this!' she'd say in a warbling voice. I asked her what the sky had been like. Sometimes she'd say, 'There was no black smoke.' Sometimes she'd say, 'Even when it was cloudy, the sky was clear with no smog.' Sometimes she'd say, 'The smoke didn't choke you back then.' Sometimes she'd say, 'There were far more blue sky days each year.' And sometimes she'd say, 'You'd see all kinds of birds flying through the sky, not like these days when you don't even see a crow.' In short, her answers were all very simple.

Our second clash was brought on by one of these bouts of coughing. She was loosening soil in the plant pots when suddenly she started to cough. I suggested that she pull out all the herbs as I'd heard that cultivating herbs over-excited the central nervous system, inducing asthma and making it hard to breathe. 'I don't grow herbs in the house,' Ji Lianna said. '*He* finds them unclean.'

'Oh, *He* doesn't exist! Not in this world! Unless he's a real elitist snob!' I said with a laugh. Corrupt officials spent all day feasting and enjoying relaxed lives, while unskilled poor people suffered lives of hardship, tormented at every turn, I ranted. Take me, for example, 24-years-old, and in fulltime work for three years, but no house to show for it, no one to look after me, unable to afford nice clothes, and with no idea how top-end restaurant food tastes. I had no disposable income to travel with; in fact I'd never even left the province. Compare this to my university classmate, the one whose father was an official, who was offered a good job as soon as she'd graduated, and when she married, she was given a house and a car. When this girl went shopping for clothes, it was to malls like New World, Parkson, Songlei or Broad, whereas I went to the Hexing Road Wholesale Clothes Emporium or to night market street stalls. When other people read newspapers, they focused on happenings between movie stars, pop concerts, new beauty products or the latest celebrity household goings on, whereas I zoned in on adverts for discounted promotional merchandise. Girls like me, the type who came from humble backgrounds and weren't great beauties were like the Second World War Jews of our age, being pushed along by an invisible force, being cleansed. That's why I didn't believe that there was a God in this world, that's why I didn't believe in *Him*.

What an idiot I was. Whenever I got myself worked up, I'd blurt out all these things I knew I shouldn't say. Despite the fact that my life had been far from ideal,

I really shouldn't have been venting my spleen against a weather-beaten old lady. I apologised to her, and told her I was certain to go to hell. Ji Lianna put down her trowel. 'If you don't have *Him* in your heart, how can you believe in hell?' she asked gently. 'People who don't know true hell can't know that there's a heaven for them either.' She turned off the living room light and felt her way through the darkness back to her bedroom. Very soon, I heard the chanting of prayers from inside. This was the second disagreement between Ji Lianna and me, and it led me to my third romantic relationship.

3

Ji Lianna gave me the cold shoulder for a number of days after that. After leaving the office, I would grab a bite to eat outside and then loiter around, braving it out until nine o'clock, which was generally the time she went to bed, before going home.

To keep safe, I spent my evenings hanging out in Central Avenue or Qidaling Park, mainly busy places with plenty of people, and close to Ji Lianna's. But it was winter, and all that time spent outdoors left my cheeks feeling rasped by the cold and forced me into a mall or a cinema to seek warmth.

One evening at around twenty to eight, I found myself in a Russian handicraft shop on the bank of the Songhua River, where a lanky man was buying a pipe. He was leaning over the counter choosing it, so preoccupied that he didn't notice the pickpocket behind him, pasted against him like a gecko to a wall.

I possessed a natural sensitivity towards mall thieves. Like me, they were not there to buy things, but while

I just gazed aimlessly around, their gaze was on other shoppers. The man buying the pipe had a grain-beige polyester backpack slung across him, and before he'd paid for the pipe, the thief slit his backpack and snatched out his wallet. With the wallet in hand, he strolled towards the door, acting as if nothing had happened. 'Thief! Catch him!' I yelled, and reached out to grab hold of the scoundrel. He looked about seventeen, not particularly tall and very slim with bleached blond hair. He wasn't wearing a scarf and I saw a tattoo of a spider on his neck. I sensed that this spider spent all day long sucking at his blood, hence why he was so pale and weak-looking. The boy was desperately trying to get out of my grasp so he could run away, but before he could, the man buying the pipe realised he'd been robbed. He launched at the boy like a sparrowhawk, and together we managed to subdue him.

The thief knelt down in front of us and begged for mercy. His father was dead, his grandfather blind, his mother paralysed, while his little sister had leukaemia, he told us. His family was poorer than poor, and didn't have money to see the doctor or to buy food; he'd had no choice but to drop out of school and do this. Thieves often lied when they got caught, wishing all of the world's disasters upon themselves just to get sympathy. As soon as he realised what was happening, the shop's security guard rushed over and called the police to report it. As soon as the police arrived, I saw a smile appear on the thief's face. The policeman asked a few basic questions about what had happened, returned the lanky man's wallet, and then led the thief away. As the thief was leaving the crime scene, he fixed me with a harsh glare, and in an aggressive voice said, 'When I get out, I'm going to fuck you to death.'

Before I had the chance to respond, the man who'd been pickpocketed said, 'That depends on whether you're man enough to actually get it up!' The surrounding crowds burst out laughing. The lanky man and I walked out of the shop together. 'I'm Qi Deming by the way,' he said, extending a hand. 'Thank you so much! There isn't much money in my wallet, two or three hundred *yuan* at most, but I have my identity card and bankcard in there. If I'd lost my bank card I'd have had to cancel it, and I have a flight to Shanghai early tomorrow morning, and without my ID I wouldn't have been allowed to board, so that would have been a major hassle!'

'Don't even mention it,' I said. 'If you'd seen a thief stealing something from me, you wouldn't have just stood idly by and watched, I'm sure.'

Qi Deming surprised me by saying, 'Who knows!'

Feeling a bit put off, I bid him farewell, and turned to leave, with absolutely no interest in talking to him further. But Qi Deming chased after me and insisted on walking me home. 'There's no need,' I said. 'I don't live far.'

'I'm absolutely not taking no for an answer,' Qi Deming said seriously. 'I'm worried about that thief, I imagine he's already been released.'

'How could that be possible?' I asked. 'He was caught stealing. He might even be a repeat offender. He's committed a crime!'

Qi Deming gave a sigh. 'Didn't you notice? When he saw the police officer, he could barely conceal his delight. They definitely knew each other. Police and criminals live hand in hand these days. Thieves give a monthly commission to the police who have their back. It's not exactly a well-kept secret, you must have heard about it. Even if you haven't, you must have got a whiff of booze on that policeman's breath? God knows who he'd just been drinking with. There's no way you could trust a man like that!'

'If they release him, I'll just have to catch him at it again and send him back. Thieves all have their turf, don't they? He'll come back here and try it again. He won't get away with it in front of my eyes though,' I vowed, stamping my foot.

Qi Deming started laughing. 'They behave just like cadres, rotating after a certain time period, moving to a new beat to keep safe, so don't think you can go around like a plainclothes cop! When the police took off with the thief, as the victim and witness we should have both been taken too, so we could file a report,' he said in an attempt to convince me. 'Our testimony was essential to prove that he'd committed the crime. The fact that they weren't following normal robbery protocol and wrapped the matter up so quickly is absolute proof that the two of them were up to something.'

I listened speechlessly as Qi Deming went on to suggest that the thief might even have a partner. And if this partner had been at the scene during the arrest, he might decide to follow me, waiting for an opportunity to get revenge. I might find myself in a whole lot of trouble. And that's why I should definitely let him walk me home.

'Let them come and get their revenge if they want it!' I said. 'I'm done with life anyway! As long as they don't leave me half dead, I don't mind.'

Qi Deming's response filled me with fear: 'When they get revenge on women, it's not your life you have to worry about, but your maidenhood!' I was so scared by this that I submitted and allowed him to walk me home. On the way back Qi Deming received two phone calls.

'Boss, you've explained that twice now. I'm not a child,' he said, a little impatiently, after picking up the first. 'Just relax, I have a plan – I won't get duped. Tomorrow I'll go to Shanghai and as soon as I have something to report, I'll call you!' He put the phone down and mumbled, 'Men get menopausal too, it seems. What a waste of time.' He appeared very pleased to receive the second call, a good friend I gathered, as he proudly boasted about how lucky he'd been that evening: he'd been in the Russian handicrafts shop when a young guy had stolen his wallet. As luck would have it there'd been a girl at the scene who had grabbed the pickpocket and he'd managed to get his wallet back without even a penny missing. 'Everyone says that it's meant to be a hero who rescues a beautiful girl,' he joked, 'but old Qi Deming is so lucky, he has the beautiful girl rescuing him!'

Qi Deming's phone manner reminded me of that of Song Xiangkui, my most recent ex-boyfriend. Song Xiangkui worked as a civil servant for a government department office. Each time his boss called, he'd stop and stand deferentially on the spot, even if he happened to be walking down the street at the time, wearing a big grin on his face as he listened. When he responded to his boss the words I'd heard most from him were: 'Yes sir, of course sir, you relax, I'll see to it.' Song Xiangkui may have acted in this servile way to his boss, but with lower-ranking colleagues it was another story. He was the section chief, and one time when we visited Zhaolin Park to see the ice lanterns, we bumped into a subordinate employee from his section. When the guy greeted him, Song Xiangkui stood up straight, and muttered some perfunctory greeting, acting like the important guy. I told him off for being so unfriendly towards his colleague, but he retorted that the government office was a place where pawns were cultivated level by level. He acted as a pawn to those above, while those below him had to be his pawn, otherwise he'd suffocate. While we were arguing, his colleague raced breathlessly back over. He'd run back to the park's entrance to buy us each a stick of candied fruit. Song Xiangkui took his stick, and waited until the guy was some distance away before smugly saying, 'Do you get it now? It's not that I want him to be subservient to me. Because he's my subordinate, he does it willingly.'

I wouldn't take the stick of candied fruit from Song Xiangkui. To me, it looked like a chain of blood-red teardrops. In a fit of rage, Song Xiangkui ate both sticks. Looking at the lanterns was meant to be a bright and hopeful experience. Who could have known that the date would end up darkening our moods so much that we would be left feeling despondent?

Qi Deming hadn't sounded humble and submissive to his boss, which gave me increased respect for him. 'So you have a government office job, do you?' I said, once he'd ended the second phone call.

'How did you know?' Under the soft streetlight, he cheekily stuck out his tongue. 'How do you think I get away with being so disrespectful to my boss!'

I smiled and said nothing, and he didn't ask any more questions. As we passed Modern's ice cream parlour, Qi Deming suddenly stopped. 'Why don't I treat us both to an ice cream?' he said.

Modern was renowned for its ice cream. There were over ten different flavours, and the texture was divine. Even in winter, you'd find Harbiners standing out in the cold wind eating ice cream, and it had turned into one of the great wonders of Central Avenue.

There were two sets of couples standing outside the parlour eating ice cream. One couple had bought one to share, him taking one bite and her the next, making passersby green with envy. The other couple had bought one each, but the girl's face was filled with such delight as she snuggled inside the boy's embrace, looking as if his chest would protect her from both, the cold from the ice cream and the cold wind. After I'd finished my ice cream, my whole body began to shake, but Qi Deming hadn't yet had his fill, and ordered another. He'd been weaned too early, he explained, and eating ice cream was like being back with his mother! So as not to keep us out any later than necessary, he ate it as we strolled.

By the time he'd finished, we were back at mine. He stood under the hazy streetlight, and glanced up at my building. 'Do you own your apartment?' he asked in surprise. I shook my head, I rent a room, I explained. 'Ah', he said. He urged me to be vigilant when I went out, and to call him immediately if I noticed I was being followed by the thief. He reached into his pocket, pulled out a name card file, and plucked out a card for me. He watched as I went inside.

It was just past nine when I got in. As I walked into my room, before I'd changed into my nightgown, I heard Ji Lianna come out of her bedroom. She opened the front door, closed it again and with a rustle I heard her relock it. She often relocked the door after I'd locked it. I wasn't convinced it was just because she thought I was careless, she was also worried because I was a stranger. Even though I was a houseguest, deep in her heart she still seemed to consider me an intruder, one she needed to remain watchful of.

I decided it was time to move out. Just because I was living in an old house didn't mean I was living the dream.

I couldn't ask for Huang Weina's help this time; the fact that I was choosing to leave a charming European-style house where I could live rent-free would definitely lead her to say that I needed to get my head checked.

But finding a place to rent really wasn't a straightforward process. I couldn't afford a place of my own, not even a one-bed. If I wanted to live within the second ring road, it would cost between 1200 and 1300 per month, which was half my salary. And with flat-shares, either the area wasn't great, it was too expensive, or the flatmates seemed untrustworthy. I spent a lot of time looking, with little to show for it. Just as I was starting to feel hopeless, Qi Deming popped up again.

That day there was a huge snowstorm, and the whole city was clogged up with traffic. After leaving work, I ate a half-dozen fried buns before starting to walk back towards Ji Lianna's. It got dark early during the Harbin winters, but the falling snow seemed to extend the daylight. The inner city lights shone onto the snowy ground giving off a white glow, illuminating the pedestrians' faces. My workplace was beneath Jihong Bridge, only two bus stops from Ji Lianna's. Even if it hadn't been snowing, and the buses were relatively empty, I would decide to walk all the same. It was the third snowfall of the season, if I remember correctly.

The snowflakes had acclimatized to the cold ground, and were not as soft as when they first started falling; they gained an unstoppable momentum and began to fall uninhibited. I liked the snow; I didn't have more than a couple of friends I felt truly close to, but when the snow was flying around, it felt like a crowd of wonderful companions had come down from heaven. They had no gripe with me, they wouldn't make false claims, they didn't mock me, they just gently kissed my face, and it felt like a small heavenly light shining. The experience filled me with joy, lifting the burdens of my mind and relaxing me. I wanted to enjoy these snowflakes for as long as I could, and was willing my journey home not to end.

'Hey there, Miss . . . ' Just as I was crossing the street, and heading towards the small European building, a man greeted me. As I approached, I saw that it was Qi Deming. He was standing at the roadside wearing a white padded jacket and looking like a lamppost. A red glow was coming from the cigarette in his hand, which he put out when he saw me. 'I've smoked three cigarettes while I've been waiting for you,' he said. 'Why are you back so late from work?'

'I ate dinner before coming home,' I explained. 'I rent a room here, but I'm not allowed to cook.'

'Your landlord must be very mean not to even let you use the gas. If you pay your share of the bills, what's the problem?' He sounded indignant, and then as if we were old friends he said, 'You may have eaten, but waiting for you all this time, my stomach's almost caved in from hunger. Come and sit with me for a bite!'

'My treat,' he added quickly when I didn't respond. My reticence had indeed been due to my empty wallet.

'I have to be back home by nine,' I said.

'Does your landlord go to sleep that early?' he asked, smiling. 'In the south, the evenings start at nine.'

We approached the typhoon shelter. Perhaps everyone was having transport trouble due to all the snow that night, and that was why the simple restaurant, usually thriving, only had a handful of customers. Qi Deming ordered fried crab, steamed chicken with chilli, chicken feet with black bean sauce and a salted meat clay-pot. 'Comfort food,' he explained. 'If I am feeling down, all I need is a good meal of comfort food and the clouds would clear and the sun would shine.' I told him I was the same as him. Even though I was still full from all those buns, I was unable to withstand the temptation of all the delicious food, and picked up a pair of chopsticks. Qi Deming commented on how cold it was and ordered a bottle of heated rice wine. We chatted as we ate.

Qi Deming told me he'd been on tenterhooks about me the whole time he'd been in Shanghai, and whenever he received a call from an unknown number he thought it must be me calling for help. It was only when he got back from his business trip and I still hadn't called, that he reassured himself that thief hadn't gone out seeking revenge. But today when it started snowing, he suddenly had a strange thought – what if the thief had killed me? That would also have resulted in my silence. He'd been really worried about me, but without my phone number, he'd had no way of getting in touch except by turning up outside my place and waiting.

'You didn't throw my name card away, did you?' he asked.

'Of course not,' I said truthfully. 'I actually started dialling your number once, I was going to ask for your help with something, but halfway through I thought you'd probably have forgotten who I was, and so I didn't call in the end.'

Qi Deming put down his chopsticks and wiped the corner of his mouth on a napkin. 'What was the problem?' he asked, looking at me.

'I saw from your name card that you're the deputy manager of a pharmaceutical research company. I imagine you must come across a lot of people, so I was wondering if you could help me find a room to rent. I'm looking for something between five and six hundred a month with a decent landlord in an area that isn't too far out.'

'If you hadn't grabbed back my wallet from that thief, I wouldn't have been able to go to Shanghai the next day,' Qi Deming responded eagerly. 'And if I hadn't gone to Shanghai, I would have missed out on the chance to sign a big order, so I really do owe you. You leave your request with me, I'll help you find a place.' He took down my phone number and told me he'd call as soon as he had news.

By the time we emerged from the typhoon shelter, the snow had stopped. Qi Deming offered to walk me home, and I didn't disagree. There weren't many people on Central Avenue, and the road seemed wider because of it. On snowy days, God became a painter, using his brush to whiten every inch he could reach. We were almost at mine when Qi Deming held his watch up to the streetlamp to check it. 'It's ten minutes to nine, I hope your landlord won't tell you off.'

'She won't tell me off, she'll just ignore me,'

'I bet she's a bitter, ugly, old landlady.'

I laughed and waved at him. I tiptoed inside, turning on the porch light and changing into my slippers. I went into my room to discover that Ji Lianna had left a bowl of steaming hot ginger soup on my desk, along with a note in my jotter pad that read: *Xiao'e, the snow is falling and it's cold so please have some of this ginger soup. The days are getting shorter and you should start to come home earlier.* Her writing was elegant and slender, curled, like musical notes.

That cup of ginger soup and the words *come home* kept me there by Ji Lianna's side.

4

I met my first boyfriend during the third year of university. It had been my dorm mates who coaxed me into getting together with him. To be honest, the girls saw him as second-rate, and that's why they thrust him onto me. 'We're already in third year, and you still haven't ever had a boyfriend, Zhao Xiao'e!' they all said. 'What's the point of four years at university if you are not dating?' So, like archaeologists they searched high and low for this relic, and Wang Ke was what they managed to dig up.

I didn't even know which department Wang Ke studied in or what his major was, but as soon as I heard his name, I shook my head, saying if I were to marry him, that would make me Mrs Wanker, and I really couldn't stand for that! Nothing wrong with masturbation, one of the young girls lectured me, at least it showed that he had sound sexual functionalities. Would I prefer being with someone who had no desire? This made everyone in the dormitory laugh until their stomachs hurt.

Wang Ke and I were at the same school of study, but he

was in the philosophy department. He was also a third-year student, but a year younger than me. He came from the south. When I asked him what province, he bit his tongue and gave the pompous response, 'South of the Yangtze.' There were lots of places south of the Yangtze, us girls heckled, could he be more specific? He continued to bite his tongue, saying, 'We all come from the same dust and soil. What's the difference if it's east, west, north or south?'

I was five foot one to Wang Ke's five three, and we were both very slight. I had small eyes, a sharp jaw, and slightly frizzy hair, and so did Wang Ke. Even our complexion was similar – cheeks that looked as if they had a sheet of yellow paper pasted over them and at a glance you could tell we were undernourished. Wang Ke and I both came from the countryside. His parents had a plot of household land they worked, while his brother, Big Wang, had left for the city to find work, and was paying for his little brother's studies through his earnings. My parents had both been uneducated, and just like him, the only reason I was at university was because my big brother provided for me – mine through his delivery work. So, Wang Ke and I both shared a deep affection towards our brothers.

My financial constraints meant I would always leave the canteen with the cheapest food, and use the cheapest toothpaste, washing powder and sanitary pads. When my clothes got holes in them, I would stitch them up and continue to wear them. I was terrified of falling sick and not having the money for medical treatment so I got into the discipline of jogging regularly, and during my four years at university I barely suffered even a cold. Meanwhile, my grades were always high. Wang Ke was the opposite of me in all these respects – he didn't like sports, saying that if people went jogging around his hometown everyone would think they were crazy – why would you run unless there was an emergency! He worked very hard, but only ever got mediocre results, and every semester there would be courses he'd fail. He regretted choosing philosophy, a major he claimed was meant to nurture sages and keepers of truths, not dimwits like him.

Wang Ke was slow-witted, and said it as he thought it; his lack of guile causing my dorm mates a lot of mirth. Like the time Li Ling asked him, 'Do you think I look good in bright clothing?' to which he replied, 'It doesn't matter how you dress, you'll never look as impressive as a peacock.' And when Zhang Yingmei asked, 'Do you prefer Nietzsche or Heidegger?' and he answered, 'I don't like either. In fact, reading their books leaves my brain feeling scrambled.' My roommates would start laughing as soon as he arrived and wouldn't stop. They'd all be very attentive towards him, letting him have their chairs and giving him things to eat – bananas, fruit jellies, milk or biscuits. As he was eating these treats, Wang Ke would give me an uneasy look, like a pitiful little child might, worried he was embarrassing me.

He knew I wasn't getting enough nutrients and one time when he was given a Fuji apple, he took a couple of bites out of necessity, but then hid the rest in his pocket. After leaving the dormitory, he pulled me into a little forested area on campus and took out a small penknife. He scraped off his tooth marks, and brought the apple up to my mouth. Even though he couldn't afford fruit, he never went without it, he told me. On the campus benches and lawns you often found half-eaten apples and pears dropped by students from wealthy families. He always carried a penknife around and whenever he found one he'd peel off the skin and eat what was left. His words and that piece of apple – over half – brought tears to my eyes.

'Wang Ke, I am yours for life,' I told him.

He panicked, and with a frown he said, 'Why is such a large person giving themselves to me? You must be all of seven stone, how am I going to keep you alive and healthy and well fed?'

I listened to this, not knowing whether to laugh or cry.

Wang Ke and I broke up after around six months together. He returned from his hometown after Spring Festival that year and started to act distant. 'Do you have a new girlfriend?' I asked him.

He told me the truth: he'd taken a photograph of me back home during Spring Festival to show his parents, who'd become so anxious they'd been unable to enjoy the festivities. They didn't like how scrawny I was, how small and thin my face was – unlucky apparently – and they'd said that my hip bones looked too narrow, which could lead to birthing complications. With great awkwardness Wang Ke explained that although he was deeply attached to me, filial piety was everything. He could choose not to get married, but he couldn't go against his parents' wishes. So that was it; we broke up, amicably enough. I prepared to take my graduate studies exams, while Wang Ke, tired of university life, decided he would head back to his hometown as soon as he'd received his graduation diploma.

We were still attending the same university, but once we'd split up and no longer made plans to meet, we were like two planets, seemingly travelling on the same path, but actually each in our own orbits, and for three whole months we didn't cross paths once. Wang Ke graduated as he'd intended, while I failed my graduate studies exams, followed by the civil service ones. The night before Wang Ke left Harbin, he invited me to Sun Island Fishing Village to dine on fish. He drank a half bottle of rice wine over dinner and as soon as we left the restaurant, he pulled me over to the lilac bush, hugging me as he wept, saying, 'Life is so hard,' over and over again, until in the end my face had become a mess of his tears and snot.

We took the last bus back, and as it crossed the bridge over the river back downtown towards campus, he handed me a thick envelope, telling me not to look inside until he'd left Harbin. I went against his instructions, tearing open the envelope as soon as I got back to my dormitory. Inside I found a stack of *Renminbi* notes of different denominations, there were a hundred *yuan* notes, as well as small ones like ones and twos. I counted out 900 *yuan* in total, before reading the letter, in which Wang Ke wrote: *Xiao'e, I'll always remember the evening beneath the white birch tree. I know I've let you down. This is money I saved by scrimping on food. It's not much, but I've heard that you can go to the hospital and have an operation to repair your hymen. If you do that, you'll still be able to find yourself a good husband.* I thought about that late summer evening, the two of us in the silver birch forest on the campus, the place where we'd consumed those forbidden fruits. It had been the first time for us both, and we were nervous and flustered. To make matters worse, there was a mouse on night-watch duty who suddenly scuttled across, scaring us senseless, and (the whole affair) made me feel no uninhibited gush of pleasure. Afterwards, Wang Ke was terrified I might be pregnant, and it was only after a month of being on edge, when my period arrived right on schedule, that he breathed a sigh of relief.

He wrote a four-stanza poem to commemorate our night:

You look at the stars in the sky
I look at the stars in your eye
The stars in the sky are like your gold ring
The stars in your eyes are my belt buckle

Wang Ke's romantic poem was so full of bright silliness that I laughed until tears streamed down my face.

As Wang Ke was departing, I rushed to the noisy train station with the 900 *yuan* to hand back to him. As we were saying goodbye, Wang Ke suddenly turned to me. 'When you've put some weight on, and filled out a bit in your face and backside, make sure to send me your photo,' he said eagerly. 'I'll get my parents to take another look.'

After hearing that, I couldn't make myself turn my head for him as he left. Who would turn their head for a boy like that!

I passed my exams in the end, and applied for a job at the Harbin Citizen Post, which boasted a decent circulation. I initially applied for a journalist position, but the day I turned up to report to work, the director told me that a proofreader had gone on maternity leave and asked if I would cover her for the time being. In the world of the newspaper, proofreaders were basically the cleaners, and not particularly respected. But I liked the job. Because I was good at picking up typos, while the thought of dealing with all those different interviewees made my head spin.

When the proofreader who I was covering for returned from maternity leave she was transferred to another position, leaving me firmly installed in my proofreader role.

Huang Weina was a journalist whose flair for words was unmatched in the newspaper, and reading over her manuscripts was a breeze, with hardly any mistakes jumping out at me. Addressing Huang Weina in front of a crowd of journalists once, I said, 'If all the journalists in this newspaper were like you, I'd be out of a job. Your manuscripts could be taken straight to the printers.' From this point on, Huang Weina and I became good friends. I remember telling her about my first love. She had a cigarette in her mouth. 'Fuck, that little weedy Wang Ke – how dare he ditch you!' she said coarsely. 'Give me that kid's address and I'll get our logistic company to deliver a fat sow to his door with the message: *Your bride has arrived,* disgust the hell out of him!'

Straight after moving in with Liu Qin, I met Song Xiangkui online. We started chatting on QQ Messenger, and sensing that we were well suited, decided to meet up in person. Song Xiangkui had a round face, small eyes, a flat nose and thick lips; a look that made him seem immediately trustworthy. When he first saw me, he noisily sucked in his lips and said, 'Well, you're a bit smaller than I was expecting.' He was referring to my skinniness.

I responded with an equally impolite, 'As are you!' Song Xiangkui was short and plump with a beer belly.

'I guess that makes us a good match,' he said cheerfully.

Song Xiangkui was also from a county outside Harbin. He worked for a government office, and had a higher status and salary than me. Logically speaking, he should have been able to rent a one-bedroom flat, but instead he lived in a flat-share. Song Xiangkui's father had died some time ago and his mother was not very well. His older brother was well into his thirties and disabled, which meant he was unlikely to get married. They both lived off a small patch of poor quality land and two cows. Song Xiangkui felt sorry for his mother and brother and he scrimped and saved all he could in order to send 800 *yuan* home each month to help with their living. Song Xiangkui really was good to his family, and it was this that convinced me to be with him. I thought that if I became part of his family, he would treat me just as well.

After we'd been together three months, Song Xiangkui's flatmate went to Guangdong on business, and for those few days both of us stayed at his. I remember the first dawn we ushered in after being together. In good spirits I laid the table with the breakfast I had carefully prepared, but I noticed Song Xiangkui didn't seem to be quite as elated. It was three days later when I left his, that I learned the reason for his displeasure.

As he was walking me to the bus stop he suddenly asked, 'So who was your first time with?'

Not thinking it necessary to censor myself, I told him about my first relationship with my college sweetheart.

'Why did you break up?' he asked.

'He went back down south to his hometown and his parents didn't like how skinny I was and rejected me as a daughter-in-law.'

Song Xiangkui gave a snide laugh. 'Are you still in touch?' he asked.

'No,' I told him.

Song Xiangkui scraped a finger down my face and said, 'That's good.'

I imagined that the interrogation was over, and was surprised when we got to the bus stop, and he put his mouth against my ear and quietly asked, 'Did you have an abortion for him?'

I shook my head.

He patted my shoulder and with a laugh he said, 'It appears that not all seeds sprout then.'

I felt angry about the way Song Xiangkui had spoken and behaved towards me; I hadn't expected him to care so much about a thin layer of skin. It seemed that Wang Ke had been right to be concerned – who understood men better than men? I started to feel estranged from him, while he acted as if nothing had happened, continuing to send text messages every day as usual, asking how things were going. When I didn't reply, he came over to my place and banged at the door crying, 'Xiao'e, it's Song Xiangkui. Open the door!' I ignored him, and Liu Qin couldn't hear him. But Song Xiangkui didn't give up; he'd wait two days and come back again. This continued until one day, when it was raining heavily, I looked through the peephole and saw him knocking on the door, thoroughly drenched and shivering with cold. Only then did I open the door.

After dating for two years, Song Xiangkui suddenly told me he was in love with someone else. I could never have imagined that this someone might be Liu Qin. I suddenly remembered coming home from work once and opening the door to find not only Liu Qin there, but Song Xiangkui too. I'd asked him how he'd got in, and he explained that he'd come over just as Liu Qin had been taking out the rubbish and they'd bumped into each other. In reality, the rubbish had still been full that day. But at the time I didn't suspect them, because I hadn't thought that Song Xiangkui would fall for a deaf girl.

Our relationship's rupture had begun when I started yearning for marriage. Song Xiangkui and I planned to get married that spring, but we had absolutely no idea where we were going to live. My workplace couldn't assign me affordable housing, and although Song Xiangkui's workplace provided such perks, he had not been there long enough, his status was still low, and in the last few years he hadn't been offered anything. After a long discussion, we decided to live in rented accommodation for the time being and wait until affordable housing became available before getting married. But it was while deciding where to rent, that the two of us started to row.

My preference was somewhere small and fairly central, making it easier to get to work, while he had his heart set on a three-bedroom place close to the linen factory, which he explained, had much lower rent, was light and spacious, and only involved one change of buses for me to get to work. But I wasn't willing to waste two or three hours each day commuting. We argued all the time, no matter where we were or what we were doing. We could be on the street, at Liu Qin's, or in a fast food joint.

'Let's just split up and get it over with. You can live in a goddamn grave for all I care!' Song Xiangkui spat during our most vicious fight.

'I agree. I'd be better off with a ghost boy than with you!' I came back with.

'Girls like you just rot in the ground where I come from. Women should obey men!'

'So go back to where you come from, get yourself the kind of woman who doesn't rot in the ground.'

Song Xiangkui was so livid that he practically had steam and smoke seeping from his eyes. He looked like he wanted to kill me.

After that devastating fight, we became more distant. We didn't mention marriage again. When we did occasionally get together, neither of us had much to say and there was a distinct lack of affection. It was late autumn when Song Xiangkui brought up breaking up, explaining that he was in love with Liu Qin. He was tired of arguing and Liu Qin would never use words to hurt him. He saw the look of scorn on my face, and said, 'Don't you dare think that it's her house I'm after. That's not my plan.'

Before long, my rental home became their marital home. I packed up my belongings in a state of devastation, vowing to myself no more boyfriends. But fate had made other plans and it brought me Qi Deming. He phoned me up one freezing cold weekend afternoon. 'Hey, Miss, I've found a flat you can rent, would you like me to take you to see it tonight? I'll take you out for dinner too while we're at it.' I told him that my landlady and I had made our peace and I no longer needed a place. 'Well you could have told me!' Qi Deming said. I'd been just about to call him, I lied. 'What are we going to do now?' Qi Deming asked. 'I've already scheduled an appointment with the landlord. Why don't we go there anyway, and then I'll just tell them it's not for you. I'll feel bad cancelling the viewing so late in the day.' I had no choice but to agree.

The place Qi Deming took me to was in the Zhongshan Gardens residential estate in Nangang district, a high-rise block of flats facing the Majiagou River. As we were going up in the lift, I had a dizzy spell. Qi Deming saw that I was out of sorts and with concern, asked me if I was afraid of heights. 'A little,' I replied.

'Luckily it's not too high up. Only the eleventh floor,' he said.

I walked out of the lift and towards the southwest-facing grey iron gate. 'Why do you have the keys?' I asked in surprise as he pulled out a set of keys and opened the door.

He smiled, saying nothing until we were both inside. 'I'll be your landlord from now on. You don't need to pay rent. You can come and go as you please. And you don't need to sign a lease!'

I was feeling very dizzy and unsure what to do. He handed me a set of keys and led me into the kitchen. I could see a silver-grey marble stove laid out with a few plates of half-prepared dishes. Qi Deming threw me a blue and white checkedapron and winked, saying, 'You don't object, do you? I just wanted to get an idea about your cooking skills.'

Ha, I thought to myself as I put on the apron, *I seemed to have become his cook.*

5

The winter Qi Deming and I started dating, Harbin experienced more snowfall than any previous year. Snow is like a gospel for lovers, and each time it snowed, I'd tell Ji Lianna I had to work overtime and wouldn't be back that night. It got dark earlier during the winter, with the sun setting at four o'clock, clocking off work before we did. I loved being out in the snowstorm, tramping through the creamy yellow reflections of street lamps as I made my way to Qi Deming's.

Crossing Jihong Bridge and going through the busy train station led me near to the West Street Carrefour supermarket, so before each rendezvous I'd stop off there to pick up all the ingredients I needed to prepare our snowy evening feast. During December in Harbin, the temperatures dropped to minus twenty or thirty even, and as I worried the vegetables might freeze on the way, I wrapped my shopping bag in silk for the ten-minute walk from Carrefour to Zhongshan Gardens. Qi Deming liked braised pork and sweet-and-sour fish, and his favourite vegetables were spinach and tomato. While the world around me was dim and drab, my shopping bag was full of beautiful, brightly coloured produce. On these nights we'd eat, shower and then rush into bed. On snowy nights the bed felt like a giant candied jujube, sweet through and through.

Qi Deming was three years older than me, and his mother had died when he was young. He had a younger sister studying in Australia. His father had lived an eventful life, full of ups and downs. He had previously been the deputy director of a large private enterprise, but had suffered his downfall during a banquet and a heavy drinking session while hosting a few visiting merchants from the south. After three rounds of drinks, one of these merchants made a comment about how great it was doing business with north-easterners, because they were all stupid, never paid attention to small amounts of money and would sign any order, which meant there were always easy profits to be made. Qi Deming's father was furious, and their argument quickly escalated into a punch-up. Fuelled by drunkenness, his father smashed a bottle down on this merchant's head, an act that sent them both down into the pits of hell. Although the southern merchant didn't become a complete vegetable, he was mentally incompetent after the incident and felt constantly drowsy. His optic nerve had been seriously damaged during the attack as well, leaving him partially sighted. Qi Deming's father lost all the family property and possessions paying out compensation and spent four years in jail as well. After being released, he no longer had the job at his old enterprise, and had no choice but to start from scratch with his own business. He had plenty of business experience so the bank agreed to give him a loan, and he used it to start up a logistics company in

Nangang district. Three years later, he paid back the money and used the profit to start a printing factory in Daowai district. He'd gotten to know a number of criminals during his time in jail, who were having a hard time finding work and were being driven to desperation by their poverty. He felt such deep-rooted sympathy towards them that most of the employees hired by his company and factory were ex-convicts. Qi Deming told me he'd often heard his father say: 'If one is given a means to live, who'd choose to walk towards death?'

When Qi Deming spoke of his father, there was no small amount of admiration, and he visited the man once a week. When I asked if he had a stepmother, Qi Deming said, 'My father has had lots of relationships over the last few years, but he's never considered re-marrying. I don't think he's ever been able to forget my mother. Whenever I visited him in jail, the only things he ever asked of me were to do with my mother. When I went to see him in March, he reminded me to put a red chicken's egg on my mother's grave during Grave Sweeping Festival, and stick a willow branch in the ground there, as these were the things she liked. When I went to see him in the summer, he reminded me to release a lantern on the Songhua River for mother on the Fifteenth day of Lunar July, scattering a few sweet corn kernels inside as those had been her favourite – she used to call sweet corn the stars of the grains. When I visited him in prison during winter, he'd start reminding me to burn plenty of spirit money when I visited the ancestral grave during Chinese New Year, so that she wouldn't be poor up there. He cared for her so well that I never really felt that my mother had died.'

I asked him what his mother had been like and how she'd made herself so unforgettable to his father, even all this time after she'd died. Qi Deming told me that his mother hadn't been a great beauty, she hadn't ever had a job; she'd simply been virtuous. During the last stages of Qi Deming's grandfather's lung cancer, his son had been too busy with the company to care for him and had left the duty of looking after the old man to Qi Deming's mother. For more than two months, this dutiful daughter-in-law stayed by the old man's sickbed, caring for him night and day, until he calmly exhaled his last breath. Seven days after burying his grandfather, Qi Deming's mother had a sudden heart attack and died. Everyone knew it had been the exhaustion of caring for her father-in-law that had killed her. I thought that having departed in such quick succession, Qi Deming's grandfather and mother would have definitely been buried in the same tomb, but Qi Deming shook his head. 'My father hated my grandfather,' he told me. 'He said, "Did you really have to take my wife with you when you died? How selfish are you! Do you expect her to continue looking after you in the afterworld too? I can't let her die of exhaustion twice!"'

While cleaning Qi Deming's place, I discovered signs of other women. Among the pile of white shirts in the drawer of the bedroom wardrobe I saw a petite pearly-pink blouse, clearly a girl's delicate item – while on the coat rack in the entrance hall hung a pair of lady's gloves – large and unlikely to belong to the same person as the blouse. In the old toothbrush holder in the bathroom there was an intricate lake-blue butterfly hairpin encrusted with sparkling rhinestones. Qi Deming didn't evade my question; he told me he'd had three girlfriends. But he didn't tell me how they'd broken up and I had no way of guessing.

Ji Lianna eventually started getting suspicious of all the overtime I was doing. One evening after she'd finished her prayers, she came to my room and said, 'If you have somewhere better to stay, why not just move there permanently. It would be better for both of us. When you don't come back at night, even when you've told me beforehand, I hear footsteps in the night and think you must have been kicked out, and I always have to get up and check. You know full well that I don't sleep well.'

Ji Lianna's words moved me, but I still responded with a lie. 'At the end of the year it gets very busy at work, and alongside my proofreading, I have bits of editing to do, and often have to work late. It will get better after New Year.' I heard myself stutter and felt my cheeks turn red as I said this.

Ji Lianna coughed. 'Each time you come back after working late you smell different!' Qi Deming was a heavy smoker, and spending time with him felt like being stuffed inside a chimney. Ji Lianna had a very long and upright nose, which I understood worked just like a polygraph machine, her senses still as quick as those of a youngster.

I lowered my head. 'I'm so sorry, Ji Lianna . . .' I began quietly.

'What does he do?' Ji Lianna asked, matter-of-factly.

I had no choice but to tell her the truth. 'He works in sales for a pharmaceutical manufacturer.'

'Are you scared of getting sick when you're older and not being able to get medicine?' After saying this, Ji Lianna gave a gentle smile and once again forgave me.

I knew that after turning seventy, Ji Lianna no longer visited the doctor and only very occasionally took medicine. She was putting her life into *His* hands, she said. But I was still young, and young people liked to put their lives in the hands of other people, even if these were often the wrong hands.

I didn't want to leave Ji Lianna's place; Qi Deming and I hadn't known each other for long and things had moved along quickly, only time would tell if it was meant to be. After all, he was better than me in every way. I was afraid that one day, just like Song Xiangkui, he would suddenly up and leave.

From that evening, every few days Ji Lianna would explain a passage from the Hebrew scripture, probably thinking that she needed to sprinkle me with these cleansing stories to cure my murky aura. With my ears constantly filled with the Biblical stories, I actually dreamed about Moses one night. He was standing there, half-God and half-man, dressed in silver robes, with hair like a torrential waterfall. His robes were as gentle, clear and bright as the moonlight, while his hair was as warm and bright as sunlight. His mouth was spurting a constant flow of cool and refreshing spring water. Ji Lianna was pouring milk out of a jug when I told her about my dream, and she seemed so shocked by it that she missed the glass and poured milk over the table.

The same weekend as I dreamed about Moses, Qi Deming was heading to Lanzhou on a business trip. Imagining the expansive north-western sands, I went out to buy him a bright blue fleece and told him to wear the extra layer when it got cold. The night before he set off, I opened his suitcase to put the fleece inside, whereby I noticed some items in there that caused me huge dismay: a box of condoms and a shroud.

I didn't know it was a shroud at first. I just saw an item of colourful satin clothing within the suitcase's nylon net layer. It wasn't this piece of clothing that upset me, but the condoms. However, I felt too devastated to ask him straight out about them, so I brought up the garment instead, and used it to steer the conversation towards his suitcase, hoping that he would intuitively offer me an explanation.

'Qi Deming, why is there a satin garment in your suitcase?' I asked him casually. 'That's what they dress dead people in, isn't it? Aren't you afraid of looking like a rotten corpse?'

Qi Deming had just finished shaving. He walked out of the bathroom stroking his chin, sniggered and said, 'Zhao Xiao'e, do you want to see it? I must warn you that one of my previous girlfriend's was so freaked out by it that she ran off.'

Even if it was Pandora's Box, I had to open it and have a good look all the same. I unzipped the suitcase's net layer and lifted it out.

It was a very large baggy gown. It had an apricot-orange background printed with green dragons and colourful clouds. Instead of buttons it had a bright yellow belt drawn around the waist, which made it look like the robes monks wore. This was his shroud, Qi Deming told me. On his nineteenth birthday, he'd visited the shroud shop and had it tailor-made. That year had been a leap year, the best time to get a shroud as it increased longevity, he explained. In the past, only the emperor was allowed to have dragon designs on his shroud, but now commoners could too, he said self-deprecatingly. This showed that society was improving; equality might still be an issue among the living, but among the dead it had been resolved.

I wasn't like his previous girlfriend who ran away because of the shroud, but I did feel a burst of nausea, the sensation that I was holding the clothing from a rotten corpse excavated from a 1000-year-old tomb in my hands. I threw it down and ran to the bathroom to vomit.

Later, Qi Deming told me that he'd thought it was glimpsing the condoms that had given me such a strong physical response; he couldn't believe that the sight of a shroud could make a girl sick. Qi Deming followed me into the bathroom, rubbing my back as he explained, 'In my line of work whenever you go to another city to discuss business deals and sign contracts, you're forced to celebrate. Once you've eaten and drunk your share, you can't avoid going to the bathhouse and getting with a prostitute. In this life you often have to do things you don't want to. And in this situation, it's impossible to refuse. As soon as you've finished the act, you forget it. It's the same situation as with my father; no matter how many young girls he sleeps with, my mother is the only one he loves. I wear those condoms to protect myself, because I feel responsible to you. But if it disgusts you, you can always walk away.'

'Would you still do this, even if we got married?' I asked stupidly as I vomited violently through my tears.

Qi Deming gave a laugh, but didn't answer my question. Instead he lit a cigarette and started to explain why he'd prepared a shroud when he was still so young and got into the habit of taking it away with him when he went on trips. He told me there was more and more chaos in the world – arising from society, natural and man-made disasters and these were hard to foresee. Someone might deliberately blow themselves up on a bus for example, there were security risks on metro escalators; obstructed fire escapes in hotels and inns; an ever-increasing number of people driving while drunk or under the influence of drugs; fake alcohol being served in more and more restaurants; regular occurrences of robbery and assault; an unprecedented number of earthquakes; while our increasingly fast-paced lifestyles and polluted environment caused our cardiovascular systems to become weaker and weaker, so much that it was common to see people drop down dead in the street. These death-inducing factors wove together, explained Qi Deming, creating an invisible net, which threatened us all constantly. All that needed to happen was for us to become wrapped in one thread, and we'd be dragged off to kingdom come.

'But even if you have an accident and die while you're travelling, how will people know to dress you in your shroud? Surely you don't have it on you whenever you go out? And even if you were carrying it when you happen to die, who'd actually know it was a shroud? And who'd be willing to put it on you?' My teeth were chattering as I said this.

'You don't need to concern yourself over this, I have it all planned out,' he explained.

'If you are in a fire or a plane crash, the shroud will burn to cinders along with you. You won't be able to wear it then. And what if your suitcase got lost when you checked it in, and your shroud went missing with it?' I asked.

'Get out, crow mouth!' Qi Deming roared, flinging his cigarette at me like a crazy man.

I put on my coat as I backed away, saying, 'You're the one who's prepared himself a shroud, how can you call what I'm saying inappropriate?'

Qi Deming didn't utter a sound. For that moment his eyes looked like they were on fire; blood, blood red.

It was ten to nine by then and there was no way I'd make it back to Ji Lianna's before nine. I suddenly wanted to try a cigarette. I went to the little corner shop outside his building to buy a packet of cigarettes and a disposable lighter before walking along the underpass to the entrance of the underground swimming pool.

I discovered that I wasn't the only one who liked that warm underpass; the stray cats did as well. Three ghoulish-looking cats were curled up on the ground under the pale white light. They lifted their heads when they heard me, and stared with shining round eyes, as if in protest at my invasion of their territory. I thought they must be starving, so I took out the half packet of popcorn I had in my bag, but they just licked at it and then turned up their noses. Perhaps it contained too many additives for them. They would choose a mouse over human treats any day. I smoked a cigarette while the cats played with the puffs of popcorn, patting them around like balls with their paws. One of the cats had only half a tail, but he was the one playing most energetically. I'd smoked three whole cigarettes, experienced their aroma, and thought to myself, *so that's why people smoke*. But another habit would mean another expenditure and if I happened to get addicted, my wallet would really suffer. I threw the cigarettes and lighter in the bin, planning to make my way to a local motel where I could get a room for the night. I'd just come out of the underpass when my mobile phone started ringing.

It was Ji Lianna. 'One of my curtain hooks has fallen off, Xiao'e. I can't pull the curtain tight, and there's light seeping in. I just can't for the life of me fall asleep. Can you please come back and replace the hook? It's too late to call out a handyman.'

'I'm coming right away there!' I responded, sounding like her saviour.

Ji Lianna was far from young and her legs and feet gave her trouble. At the turn of each season, she'd hire a handyman to come in and carry out tasks such as changing and washing the curtains, scrubbing the doors and windows, cleaning the ceiling, wall cabinets and anything else that involved climbing. It was that silver curtain hook falling that day that saved me from having to fork out for a night at a motel.

I arrived back at Ji Lianna's, took off my felt boots, and drank the mug of hot milk she handed me, before getting to work on the curtain hook. I carried in the stainless steel folding ladder from the balcony, set it up and with the spare curtain hook in my hand, I climbed up to the top. Ji Lianna stood at the bottom of the ladder, warning me, again and again, to be careful. The house had very high ceilings and her bedroom curtains were also a good length longer than those of most houses and very elegant. The curtains were cream with light silver floral patterns printed on them and trimmed with apricot tassels. They were beautiful, classic, European-style drapes, with a short layer of ruffled cloth between them. In my opinion it would have been fine not to draw them during winter, because the nights were long and dark, while the curtains were so heavy they were difficult to draw. The curtain hooks were made of hard plastic, the kind of material that aged like osteoporotic bones, turning brittle and becoming easy to snap. I suggested she swap them for copper hooks.

'Let's wait until Passover to change them,' Ji Lianna said.

Passover was a traditional Jewish festival, which generally fell each year at spring.

As I was coming down the ladder, I saw Ji Lianna standing on the ground. Under the soft light, dressed in her blue floral cotton nightgown, she looked like a quaint porcelain vase. How had a woman who inhabited such a delightful shell not ignited the flames of love? Huang Weina had told me that when she'd interviewed Ji Lianna she'd been able to ask about anything, except the subject of love. As soon as she broached this topic, Ji Lianna clammed up.

I went into my room and was laid out on the bed when I suddenly remembered the cigarette Qi Deming had flung at me, how it had still been lit. *What if he'd forgotten to stamp it out and had fallen into a hazy sleep while it started a huge fire?* Even though we'd broken up, I didn't want something bad like that to happen to him. I sent him a text message saying, *Make sure you've stamped out that cigarette before you drift off into sweet dreams* Qi Deming responded quickly saying, *Since being with you, there've been no damn sweet dreams!*

Lying there in the darkness, I slapped myself.

6

Most of the Jewish people living in Harbin were from Russia. After the construction of the China-Eastern railway, Jews started to flood into Harbin. Among them were skilled engineers, teachers, doctors and missionaries, but the majority were businessmen. They were clever and hardworking, and business was good. These businessmen worked in industries including animal husbandry, soybean export, shipping, milling, brewing, and the production of cigarettes, sugar and furs. After Russia's October Revolution broke out, Soviet armed guards seized power from the Tsar, intensifying the civil war. The anti-Semitic storm got worse and worse, with unbearable abuse being unleashed on some Jews, who fled to China via Siberia. It was at this time that Ji Lianna's mother arrived in Harbin along with her father, Ji Lianna's grandfather. Ji Lianna's mother was six months pregnant with her at the time. Ji Lianna's father had been a master violinmaker and was stoned to death in Yekaterinburg.

Ji Lianna was born at the beginning of the 1920s, a time of flourishing trade in Harbin. Her grandfather was a shoemaker and her mother was a nurse. After arriving in Harbin, her grandfather found work in a tannery, continuing his original line of work, while her mother started working at a Jewish women's charitable trust. They often took Ji Lianna to the theatre, but while other people were delighted to be there, the experience put Ji Lianna's family in low spirits. It was only when she was older that Ji Lianna realised her grandfather and mother only used to take her there to pay tribute to her father, who had been passionate about music.

When she was five, Ji Lianna started dance training, and at seven, she started to study music. When she was ten, her mother remarried. Ji Lianna's stepfather was also Jewish, from Poland. The construction of the Chinese-Eastern Railway began and a vast number of railroad ties were needed. Her stepfather sensed an excellent business opportunity and went into timber trading, making a lot of money. By the time he and Ji Lianna's mother married, he had become a major shareholder in the Jewish National Bank. After they married, they had a son. However, while there were photos of Ji Lianna's half-brother among those on her mantelpiece, there were none of her stepfather. Ji Lianna's half-brother was her only sibling, and he had been a very handsome young man. Based on his son's appearance, I imagined her stepfather to have been a suave romantic. One of these photographs was in a different frame to all the rest; bronze textured, and diamond shaped, with cirrus cloud decor around its edges, like a musical stave. Inside it was Ji Lianna's real father.

Huang Weina told me that when interviewing her about her family, Li Lianna had talked animated about how her grandfather had got drunk and sung songs on the balcony on a summer's night; how the greedy old family cat had stationed himself by the stove while her mother was grilling fish, and got his tail singed by the flames; how the first time her brother had gone ice skating he had tumbled and smashed his front teeth. But when asked about her stepfather, she'd responded with the single indifferent comment: 'He smoked a lot of opium and came to a bad end.' He died from an opium overdose, apparently. After her stepfather's death, Ji Lianna's little brother was adopted by a widowed aunt living in America, and when he was older he ran a farm in California. He became ill and died aged forty-eight, and was buried in his beloved farm, separated by vast oceans from his parents. I noticed that when Ji Lianna used her silver silk handkerchief to dust her family photographs, she lingered over her brother's the longest, perhaps out of pity for the brevity of his life.

Huang Weina accompanied an Israeli cultural delegation to visit the Huangshan Jewish Cemetery in Harbin's eastern suburbs, where she reported to have stumbled across Ji Lianna's mother's grave. She'd found it next to her grandfather's, and some way from that of her stepfather. Huang Weina's explanation for this was that Ji Lianna's mother couldn't have ever truly loved her second husband, as if she had, she would have asked Ji Lianna to bury them together in her will.

But I thought differently. Ji Lianna had been in charge of the funeral arrangements, and if she'd despised her stepfather, there was every chance she would have deliberately flouted her mother's wishes. The way I saw it, the relationship between stepparents and stepchildren forced two unrelated tributaries to convene into the same river. The lucky ones would find a way to either break free or blend together, while the unlucky ones would run their own paths, having nothing to do with each other. This was something I understood well.

I was born in a small village near to Keshan, where the soil was incredibly fertile and abounding with potatoes. The pure water of Wuyuer River flowed through our small village, where it was treated like a washing basin, a bath-house and a food storehouse, by people who used it to wash clothes, bathe in and catch fish and shrimps from. My father was the accountant for the village committee, and had excellent maths skills, while my mother tilled the land. My father suffered from hyperthyroidism, which made him thin and brittle. He hated the feeling of hunger and needed food near him constantly during waking hours. He had bulgy eyes and a bushy beard, and when he was angry, I always worried that his eyeballs would pop out and drop into the ragweed of his filthy beard. He'd always rained humiliation down upon my mother and I for as long as I could remember. He'd often point at my mother's face, yelling at her, 'You bitch . . .' He hated the sight of me, and was forever pulling at my plaits and shouting, 'Little mongrel'.

My father would use any small excuse to curse and beat me, while he showed my older brother nothing but love, never raising even a finger at him, instead always making sure that he was well-fed and well-dressed, even when the rest of us went without. My brother was spoilt, but in no way arrogant, and any nice food he was given he'd be sure to share with me.

The first time I knew for certain that father and I were not related by blood, I heard it from my aunt on his side. It was my first summer holiday since starting primary school and she was visiting from Qiqihar. She was medium-build, with a pear-shaped face, small eyes, a snub nose and a wonky mouth, one corner high and the other low. Her skin was coarse like pigskin and she was unbelievably ugly. My aunt ran a stall in the night market selling cheap clothing, and she'd integrated herself into this stall by wearing her own garish ware. Our family's colourful rooster pecked her foot as soon as she arrived, probably resenting her for being more brightly dressed than him. During her visit, my aunt handed my mother 10 000 *yuan* to take me away. She knew a family who wanted to adopt me, she explained, they raised sheep and were very wealthy. Mother returned the 10 000 *yuan*.

'Xiao'e is too old to be given away,' she told my aunt.

'Who says she's too old to be given away!' roared my father. 'She's only just turned seven, she understands sod all!'

'The place you're planning to take her isn't far from Keshan,' said my mother. 'She'll remember her way back here and turn up sooner or later.'

'In that case I'll poke her eyes out. See if she can remember how to get back after that!' said my father, his fierce words scaring me to tears.

My mother calmly fetched a pair of scissors from inside and handed them to my father, saying, 'If you dare to give Xiao'e away, you'll have to blind me first!'

Father refused to take the scissors. He was so angry he was shaking. It was his own eyes he should be blinding, he said, because the biggest regret of his life was marrying my mother. He told my mother that with her fox-like face, willowy waist, peach blossom eyes, slender lips, and high cheekbones, she should have become a prostitute.

He should have listened to his own mother's advice not to marry such a beautiful, vixen-faced woman. If he had done, he would be living a peaceful and happy family life right now.

With his eyes blood red, my father yelled at my mother. 'There are so many women in the village, why did the rapist only force himself on you? It must have been that flirtatious air of yours!'

My aunt grabbed the scissors from mother's hand, and spittle flying from her mouth, she said, 'As your sister-in-law, I think I have the right to say this. It's bad blood running through Xiao'e's veins. The sooner you get rid of her, the sooner your family will find peace. As she gets older, she's likely to give you trouble.'

Mother's eyes were red as she said, 'As long as I'm still breathing, don't even think of giving her away!'

So my aunt didn't end up taking me away, but from that day on, scissors were always disappearing from our house. I'd steal them from our house and chuck them down the village latrine and mother would be forced to go out and buy yet another pair. The old man who emptied the shit from the latrines would pluck out these scissors and go round the whole village asking, 'Come on, who's the woman in this village who's dropped her scissors down the bog?' The day my mother finally realised it was my doing, she hugged me, sobbing, and told me that as long as she was there with me, nothing was going to happen to my eyes. It was only then that I gave up this habit. When I was eleven, my mother fell sick and died. As she was being buried, I stood under the scorching sun, shivering all over. Even though I knew I wasn't going to have my eyes poked out by any scissors, without my mother there with me, all the brightness had left my life anyway.

Six months after my mother died, my father remarried.

She was a young divorcée from a neighbouring village, ten years younger than my father and pretty, but frivolous and flirtatious, and too lazy to help out with work around the house or the fields. She was addicted to gambling, and if she didn't touch mahjong tiles for three days, she started getting twitchy. She and my father had only been married a fortnight, when he started complaining, accusing the matchmaker of having tricked him. According to this matchmaker's description of my stepmother, she was virtuous and capable, and of high moral character. In reality, she didn't even know the trick of adding alkaline to steamed buns to make the dough more pliable; the clothes she washed never came out bright; and most absurd of all – she was completely unable to tell the difference between seedlings and weeds. When she did actually venture out into the fields with her shovel, the plants she laid out on the field ridges ready to be replanted might very well be weeds, while those lying rotting in the ditch between the fields were probably seedlings. Our work-shy father found himself with no choice but to get out into the fields and carry out this work himself.

The worst thing was when stepmother lost at gambling and returned home in a foul mood. She wouldn't dare vent her anger on my father or brother and so it was the family dog and I who bore the brunt. She'd take a hot poker out the fire and whack it against the dog's head, yelling at him for glancing around and getting distracted when he was supposed to be guarding the house (which no dog ever did). She got furious at him for not guarding the chickens properly who managed to slip into the house as a result and jump up onto the stove, where they gobbled up most of the leftover rice (the dog was chained up, so I'm not sure how he was expected to chase out the chickens either). She yelled at me for not digging out the stove ashes promptly enough, resulting in a pithy, inadequate fire and lots of thick smoke which made her choke. She despised the fact that I always had black mud under my fingernails, which she said looked like shit and put her completely off her food. She also complained about how I ground my teeth when I slept which stopped her from appreciating the lovely chirruping cicada. So basically nothing the dog or I did was ever right. She punished the dog by starving him until he was so hungry he didn't even have the energy to howl for food, while her punishments for me were more varied. Sometimes she made me eat rancid rice. Sometimes she made me go out and catch birds from the snowy ground, saying she had a craving for bird meat. The thing that I found most intolerable was when she threw her blood-spotted menstrual pants at me and ordered me to wash them. My cotton shoes were falling apart one year, and she said she would buy me a new pair. But this never happened. One snowy day, she returned home after losing at mahjong, and told me she was going to take me to buy these new shoes, but before she did I had to stand on the scalding stove, until I'd baked the gum base off my old shoes. Before it was out with the old, there would be no in with the new. I knew that if I were to stand on the stove it would turn my feet into a pair of roast ducks, so I challenged her, saying that if she did it first, even for just one minute, I'd wash her feet for her every day. My stepmother flew at me, calling me a little bastard and yelling how dare I answer her back. She pushed me down onto the floor, and was wrenching my thigh around when my older brother arrived back. My brother picked up the hot poker she used to hit the dog and whacked it down on her back. From that point on she was more moderate with me.

She searched high and low for a girlfriend to match my brother up with. She said it was shameful that he was still living off his parents at this age; that he should be the head of his own family by now. In actual fact my brother already had a girlfriend. Her father worked in haulage and had taught my brother how to drive so he could get his licence, and he was already helping out with her family business on the sly. When they got married, his wife didn't move in with our family, as was the custom, but instead my brother moved into his father-in-law's house. This was seen as deeply shameful, and made it even harder for my father to hold his head up in public.

So, the rape of my father's first wife remained a mystery, his daughter was not his own, meanwhile his son had married into another household completely without his knowledge, and alongside all of her other negative attributes, his second wife also cuckolded him. My step-mother was obsessed with Old Yang who ran the medical clinic and every time she wanted to see him, she'd just pretend to fall ill and go for some acupuncture. Father would gnash his teeth when this happened and say, 'Go and get your acupuncture. I hope he uses those needles to stab you to death!' Stepmother didn't care; she just swept off to meet her lover.

Through overhearing things said by family members and other villagers, I gradually learnt what had befallen my mother. The same month my parents got married, my father's father died. My bereaved grandmother accused my mother of being a harbinger of death. She packed up her things and left Keshan to live with my aunt in Qiqihar, saying she wasn't ready to die yet. During the second year of their marriage, my mother gave birth to my brother. The summer my brother turned four, my father went to Harbin to attend a two-week training course in basic rural accountancy. His sixth day away coincided with the Fifteenth day of Lunar July, Ghost Festival. My mother went to visit my grandfather's grave to pay her respects, and while she was there, she was raped. No one found out about her rape until I was two, before which, father always assumed me to be his biological child. I was playing outside when a motorbike knocked me over, and I started bleeding profusely. With my life in critical danger, I needed a large blood transfusion, and it was at this point that father found out that he and I were not related by blood. By the time my life was no longer in the balance, my mother's was turned upside down. Father accused her of sleeping around with some villager, narrowing it down to three suspects: the village party secretary, Mr Zhang the veterinarian, or Mr Mou the blacksmith. One of these men had power, one had money and one had physical strength. As he saw it, it was only these three attributes that sent women off the rails. Father locked mother indoors and denied her food and drink, while he spent two days and two nights interrogating her. She said nothing. Father was furious and he took out a homemade detonator, threatening to blow up the suspect. It was only then that mother told him the truth. She said that if I wasn't his child, she must have been impregnated by the man who raped her. When she fell pregnant, mother didn't know whether I was my father's child or not, because one week after the rape, father returned home from his course in Harbin and they engaged in normal marital relations.

As soon as father discovered that I was the daughter of a rapist, he became so angry he didn't know what to do. One moment he said he was going to burn me like firewood, the next he was going to throw me into the composting latrine. A neighbour summed it up, saying overnight I'd gone from being a precious baby daughter to a piece of garbage. Once he'd stopped interrogating my mother, he took my brother to have a blood test, to see if the same applied. My grandmother was even more outraged than her son. My mother had been raped at my grandfather's graveside. She felt as if it had been her husband who'd come back to life to climb from his grave and give his limbs a stretch. Grandmother cursed her dead husband, and vowed not be buried next to him when she died, convinced that the gravesite was unclean. When I was four, my grandmother sensed she was nearing the end and decided to come back to Keshan to die. My brother told me that, just as she'd been about to die, she'd grabbed my father's hand and forlornly said, 'Please bury me next to that old thing after all. He may have let me down, but I can't do the same to him.' I was locked inside the storehouse during my grandmother's funeral, like a mouse trapped in the darkness. I wasn't allowed to be there in my mourning clothes like my brother, as my father deemed me unworthy.

Being rejected by father and the villagers was the general theme of my upbringing. When my true identity came to light, my father reported the incident to the police, even though it had happened so long before. The police came to our house to talk to my mother and get a full picture of what had happened, but she had been extremely uncooperative apparently and people started to think that she'd actually had a lover, and the rape was nothing more than a cover-up story.

When mother became seriously ill, she had called me to her bedside, where she urged me to study hard and forget what happened. Life was hard and short, she said, and you had to find a way to be happy. But how could I be happy, especially once I was old enough to understand things and had the inescapable sensation that there was filthy blood flowing through me? The hardest thing to bear was the rumour flying around the village that I was the love child of my mother and a ghost, which meant that I wasn't even human! This was because my mother had been raped on Ghost Festival at twilight, when the sun set behind the mountains and the ghosts came out.

Most people only went to visit gravesites in the mornings. Apparently mother had gone at dusk that year because my father wasn't at home to remind her it was Ghost Festival and she'd completely forgotten. It was only on her way back from digging up potatoes in the fields that she'd passed the entrance to the village, seen the big heap of ash left from the burnt up spirit money at the junction and realised that it was Ghost Festival. She'd gone straight to the grocery store to buy liquor and spirit money to take to my grandfather's grave. She'd never imagined she'd return with a ghost embryo inside her.

My father and stepmother didn't get on as well as they'd hoped and actually made each other quite miserable. His hyperthyroidism got steadily worse, and he developed tachycardia, which left him short of breath and thin as a mummy; while his face looked like an expanse of the Dead Sea, devoid of any life, apart from his bulging eyes like beacon lights. But even with those beacon lights he still went off course and in the spring that I took my university entrance exams, he hung himself. According to some, he'd been discovered embezzling public funds and had committed suicide to escape punishment, because after his death a couple of large accounts were found that didn't add up. Others said he couldn't bear the torment of being ill and having my stepmother cheating on him and he'd done it to escape his pain.

Grandmother had left a note when she died, forbidding my mother from being buried at the Zhao ancestral grave at Eastern Hills cemetery because she was unclean. So when mother died, father buried her in Western Hills, which was filled mostly with the graves of people who'd died violent deaths, died young or without children. When father died, brother wanted him to be buried by her side – they were his true mother and father after all – but I was vehemently opposed. I was scared that he'd continue to heap curses on her and humiliate her in her next life too. I threatened brother, saying that if he dared bury father in Western Hills I would dig up his grave myself. In the end, my aunt unwittingly helped me out, saying that my father was a Zhao, and as a Zhao, he should naturally be buried at the Eastern Hills ancestral grave.

While father was still in the morgue, everyone my step-mother's owed mahjong debts to came knocking at the door to collect their money. They knew that without father, there was no longer anyone bankrolling her and unscrupulously they arrived at the house to take away everything of worth. Like a plague of locusts, they scuttled toward the television, the washing machine, the bike, the rice cooker and the furniture. My aunt, who still hadn't left my dead father's side, was outraged. She picked up the ice drill used for winter fishing and like a warrior armed with a spear, she charged at the debt collectors, scaring them so much they started running for their lives. Gambling was illegal, she snarled, at them and therefore there was no such thing as a gambling debt! Whoever dared take so much as a needle and thread from her brother's house would have their brains dashed out. Stepmother was an extremely formidable character, but she was like a minnow faced with a whale when it came to dealing with my aunt. After all this, my aunt took out a certified copy of my father's will and forced my stepmother to write herself out of it, transferring everything in the house under my brother's name, and all the land under hers, leaving me inheriting nothing. This was completely expected. Whether the will was fake or real, whether father was dead or alive. I'd known how it would be, I'd known that he wouldn't want me to benefit from him, not in the slightest.

My brother was living at his father-in-law's and working in haulage and while our house was unoccupied, my aunt tried to take it over. She rented out her place in Qiqihar and she and my uncle moved to Keshan. I was worked to the bone, sowing the land in summer, fishing in winter, as well as rearing poultry. The potatoes she grew were as round and plump as she was and they sold very well. Recently my brother had phoned me in Harbin, to tell me the village was to be redeveloped. Land was being requisitioned and rebuilt and we were going to have to move from the old family house. Before the compensation amount was even announced, my aunt had informed my brother that they should split it evenly between the two of them. Her logic was simple: if she hadn't spent money on house repairs, it would have crumbled to the ground long ago. She also told my brother that if he wasn't prepared to split the compensation with her, he could repay the money she'd spent on these repairs instead and quoted 60 000 *yuan*. Seething, brother said, 'All you did was replace two windows, aunt. Are those new window frames plated gold?'

7

After leaving Keshan for university, I never spoke to anyone about my true identity. My brother urged me in no uncertain terms never to mention any of it to anyone I was hoping to become romantically involved with. Men would run a mile, he said. It seemed that being the daughter of a rape victim made me sullied by association.

I hated my biological father for plunging my mother and me into this dark place. If my mother were still alive, I would have definitely plucked up the courage to ask her in detail about what happened that night. Even though it had been twilight, before the moon had risen, it wouldn't have been pitch-black. She must have still been able to make out the shape of someone drawing close, noticed whether he was tall or short, fat or thin, the general outline of his face, his voice, even the smell of his breath. There was no way she could have been left without any impression whatsoever.

Most of the time when I was surfing the web, I was visiting local public security websites. I searched through all the photos of wanted persons the right age to be my father, checking to see whether we shared any common features.

Sometimes I fell into a trance while looking at them and actually forgot what my own face looked like. I started carrying around a small mirror, not for lining my eyebrows and applying lipstick like other girls, but so that I was able to glance at myself while looking at the men in the wanted persons' photographs and so I could compare myself to them.

I didn't think my mother's rapist would have lived too far from our village, which meant he was probably from the Keshan region. Most likely he had a relative buried at Eastern Hills; what else would he have been doing at a cemetery during Ghost Festival? I returned to my hometown during university holidays to follow up this lead, and made my way discretely to the Eastern Hills. Like a student conducting field research, I jotted down all the names I found written on those gravestones, row after row, after row. I didn't discover anything suspicious. Everyone buried there was from the village.

Having failed to come across any clues from the gravestones, I went on to the three neighbouring villages, asking if there had been any rapes there. This line of inquiry led to equally disappointing results. In the last thirty years, there had only been one criminal from these three villages: a thief, and he was younger than me.

Some nights, unable to sleep, I let my thoughts run away with me. What if I was what the villagers said I was: the child of my mother and a ghost, which would make me half-human and half-ghost. Was it when I was fast asleep that my *ghost* side surfaced? What kind of demon did I turn into? A fire fox? A green snake? A human-devouring witch? I started to associate myself with all things ghoulish and witchlike. Once when I was spending the night at Song

Xiangkui's, I dreamt I'd transformed into a huge fish, every inch of my body covered in scales. I woke up, terrified. 'Do I have scales all over me? Have a proper look!' I asked him, again and again. Song Xiangkui cast a bleary eye at me, scooped my naked body into his arms and gently said, 'You're completely smooth. No scales at all. It would be pretty fantastic if you did have scales though, I never ate such a big fish.'

But still feeling panicky, I wriggled out from his embrace and ran to the bathroom where I stood in front of the mirror, looking at my reflection. Song Xiangkui's rented apartment was old and dilapidated, but it had a decent bathroom, which was spacious, with an east-facing window. The dawn light coated the mirror in creamy-yellow sheen, and looking back at me from inside it was a beautiful young girl with bright, clear, blemish-free skin. But all the while I could feel my mouth brimming with brine and, sensing the ocean's waves surging behind me, I began weeping.

I was devastated after my bust-up with Qi Deming. Our relationship had gone from boiling to freezing point overnight, all contact severed. I tried as hard as I could not to think of him, but the week between Christmas and New Year's I started to miss him a great deal. I thought about him taking his shroud to Lanzhou and wondered if something might actually have happened to him. I went online and searched for all the accidents in Lanzhou while Qi Deming was there and the names of the people who'd been fatality injured. After eliminating the possibility that he'd died during his trip, I turned my attention to Harbin, looking up every accident that had resulted in fatalities here and filtering through them. I even got in touch with my university classmate Li Ling, who

I hadn't talked to for a long time and asked her whether Qi Deming's name was on the list of people who'd been cremated recently at Huangshan Crematorium, as her father was a cremator there.

Such deep-seated worry about your ex-boyfriend was a sure sign that you were still yearning for him. How utterly depressing.

Ji Lianna had obviously sensed something was not right between the two of us, and on the last day of December, after turning the soil in the plant pots, she strolled into my bedroom, the smell of vanilla wafting from her whole person. 'If you don't have any plans for New Year's Day tomorrow, I suggest we both go to Modern at three o'clock in the afternoon and enjoy a spot of European cuisine together, Xiao'e.'

'I'm free tomorrow. That sounds lovely,' I said.

I didn't actually like European food, and not just because of the exorbitant cost. I just found it too fussy with all those rows of cutlery lined up in front of you, with no wooden or bamboo chopsticks to make life easier. The worst thing was plunging your knife and fork into an undercooked steak and watching the blood ooze out of it. It made me feel like a surgeon holding a scalpel and the bloody mass in front of me was a diseased organ I'd just cut out. It really turned my stomach. I far preferred cheap and cheerful Chinese restaurants where they cooked home-style food.

The first thing I did on New Year's morning was go down to our little local restaurant and order myself a bowl of noodles. Next, I headed to the florist's where I bought Ji Lianna a bunch of fire-red carnations and pale yellow lisianthus. Worried the flowers would freeze, I'd worn my

colourful, thick cotton jacket and tucked the flowers inside
it, next to my chest, tying a belt round my waist so they
wouldn't fall out.

Ji Lianna noticed that my chest and abdomen had both
swelled since she'd seen me leave the house and stared at
me through wide eyes. 'Ah!' she exclaimed when I undid
the belt buckle and presented her with the flowers, 'ah
look, you've brought in the spring!'

As well as the flowers, I gave her a pair of woollen
kneepads, while her New Year's present to me was a
cerise angora scarf. She told me that this scarf would go
well with my short white jumper, which worn together
would look like red plum blossom on the snowy ground.
Ji Lianna used to be a music teacher and had also taught
painting. Painting and music were the high mountains
and rippling streams, the eternal companions, of high
culture. Roaming around the magnificent vistas provided
to her by these two art forms, Ji Lianna had soaked up so
much of their essence that she had become as elegant as a
painting or a series of musical notes. I'd never seen plum
blossom before, I told Ji Lianna. In Keshan, most of the
flowers I'd seen were the ever-present wild chrysanth-
emum and potato flowers in the fields. I told her that my
mother's grave was surrounded by wild chrysanthemums
that bloomed in yellow, white and purple. As Ji Lianna was
putting the flowers in a vase, she asked me how my mother
had died and how long ago. From an illness, when I was
eleven, I told her. 'Oh . . . ' she said, fondling the soft lisianthus petals. 'And do you have a stepmother?' she asked.
I nodded, explaining that my father had remarried, but
committed suicide not long after, following which my
stepmother had married another man and had gone

off to be someone else's stepmother. Ji Lianna looked at me pityingly, gave a sigh and said, 'The best flowers don't blossom for long . . .' Fearing she might have made me upset, she started telling me how aged nineteen or twenty she'd visited Suzhou to see the plum blossom for herself. It had been March, a time when Harbin was still covered in frost and snow, but down there it was already spring, a gentle breeze flowing through the air. It had actually snowed when she'd been at Xiangxue Hai, and she'd understood that the plum blossom orchard had not been vivid enough for *Him*, so *He*'d decided to scatter huge petals of white plum blossom down alongside it. The red plum blossom was the most striking of all the plum blossom at Xiangxue Hai, resembling lanterns; the purple plum blossom was the most elegant, like the knot-buttons on the collar of a lady's dress. But Ji Lianna explained, it was the white plum blossom that had touched her the deepest. It had been the closest to *Him*, she said. She told me that emperors Kang Qi and Qian Long had travelled south many times to enjoy the sight of this blossom and experience the divine energy of the flowers. As she was telling me about plum blossom, Ji Lianna's eyes started to well with tears. Stories that involved women and flowers were often sad tales, and I had been just about to change the subject when the old man from the reception room at work called to tell me he'd just signed for a courier parcel that had been delivered to me, and that I should come in to pick it up. So I rushed off, leaving Ji Lianna in her melancholic state.

Melancholia was a form of beauty and I decided that it would be better for Ji Lianna to appreciate this beauty alone.

My brother was the only person in the whole world who I considered to be family. Yes, I had an uncle and an aunt, but we were not in the slightest bit close. Whenever I returned to the village to visit my mother's grave I'd always stay at my brother's. I'd heard from the villagers that whenever I went back, my aunt would be on high alert. She would keep the door firmly closed, as if countering some formidable enemy and so even the poor ducks and chickens suffered, by having their freedom to run around foraging curtailed. 'Once a dog smells a bone, it won't let it go,' my aunt told people. As far as she was concerned, as soon as I had a foot in that door, I'd be like a dog with scabies, refusing to leave again. She was obviously unaware that I had no desire whatsoever to step over that threshold, that it held too many painful memories.

I phoned my brother on the way to the office to wish him a happy New Year. He didn't mention the parcel during our conversation, so I assumed it must have been sent by someone else. As my brother and I were talking, my sister-in-law interrupted to say, 'When are you going to bring your boyfriend here to introduce him to us, Xiao'e?' I told her it was early days still. Gently my sister-in-law reiterated her warning, 'Whatever you do, don't mention your past while you're getting romantically involved. Bear that advice in mind, I beg you, don't be rash and foolish.' My sister-in-law was a straightforward and kind-hearted woman, who had impressed me greatly by never once complaining about how my brother had paid my university fees. But her reminder, however kindly intended, filled me with disappointment. Walking along those streets filled with their festive atmosphere, I suddenly sensed oppressive dark clouds hanging overhead.

Never in a million years would I have guessed that I'd find Wang Ke's signature on the parcel form. We hadn't been in contact once since that day at the train station. Carrying the package into my office felt a bit like carrying a resuscitated heart. I was slightly taken off guard that he even knew where I worked.

We'd been given three days off over New Year's, and the only people left in the office were those who were on the rota to work over the holidays, which meant it was very quiet. I carried the package over to my desk, got my scissors and hurriedly cut it open. The first thing to jump out at me was a bag of dried bamboo, followed by a packet of pork jerky. My interest wasn't in the food he'd sent. I turned the package upside down, sending the contents clattering out onto my desk. Eventually I found what I was looking for: a manila envelope. It was a slim letter in an unsealed envelope. I pulled out the letter paper, which had been crushed by all the food items in the package, making it crumpled and tatty. The letter began with no salutation, and was very brief and to the point:

From asking around our university classmates, I found out that you're doing pretty well for yourself, that you have a stable job and a boyfriend too. I'm really happy for you! After graduating I got a job as an administrative officer for the township government office back in my hometown. It's not a particularly taxing job, but it's taxing on the gut – I've put on about a stone and a half and developed fatty liver too! I'm married. She is a community teacher two years older than me, not particularly attractive and rather plump, but my parents like how docile, adept and easy to please she is. We've just had a little girl, no teeth

yet. My mother wants us to have another, she won't be
satisfied until we have a son apparently and so it looks like
we might need to go against the policy! I started smoking
last year and now I'm on two packets a day. I need to
quit if we start trying for another child, but I'm finding it
impossible. When I have trouble sleeping at night, I often
smoke and think of you. Have you filled out at all? Do
you still get those split ends? I'm sending you some of our
local speciality food. Tell me which you like and I'll send
you some each year. Do you still remember my brother, Big
Wang? He bought a lottery ticket two years ago and won a
couple of hundred thousand yuan. Our whole family has
enjoyed a markedly improved lifestyle since then. If you
ever travel south for work, please be sure to take a detour to
ours and I'll show you around.

At the end of his letter, Wang Ke had written his mobile
number.

Once I'd finished reading the letter I turned my
attention to the food items, carefully inspecting them one
by one. As well as the dried bamboo and pork jerky, there
was red ginger, betel nuts, green tea, fermented black
beans and lotus seeds. The breath of Wang Ke's hometown
had infiltrated these food items and left a faint odour.
I opened the bag of red ginger, tore off a strip and put it
in my mouth. The first bite was intense, but as I chewed
it longer, it started to taste delicately sweet. These food
items, with their array of flavours and various smells,
started to make me feel nostalgic. I searched my mind
for an image of what a fat Wang Ke might look like, but
I just couldn't see it. To me he was just like that pickled
red ginger; I would never be able to rediscover his true

flavour. I scrunched up Wang Ke's letter and threw it into the wastepaper basket. I left the pork jerky, bamboo and black beans to give Huang Weina, and the rest of the items I swept back into the package to take back and share with Ji Lianna.

As I left the office, I was hit by a gust of cold wind and, all of a sudden, I was feeling miserable. The New Year's streets were bustling, decorated with lanterns and colourful banners, and full of people whose faces were brimming with joy. All the while I was crying. I was carrying the package in one hand, while wiping away my tears with the other, asking myself, 'What are you crying about!' But my tears didn't listen to reason and continued to trickle down my cheeks. Sometimes heart and body seemed like two separate entities.

Scared that Ji Lianna would see that I'd been crying, I stopped off at a supermarket first and went to the ladies. Only after washing my face and calming myself down did I return home.

It had just gone noon and Ji Lianna was in her room praying. I took the package into the kitchen and boiled a pot of water. I let it sit for a couple of minutes to cool before opening the packet of green tea Wang Ke had sent me and brewing a pot of it. Next I took out the red ginger and the betel nuts, placing two pieces from each onto a little saucer, and carrying it all over to the little dining table next to the piano. After she finished her noon prayers, Ji Lianna liked to sit there and enjoy a cup of tea.

That was the first time I'd ever prepared tea and refreshments for her.

I returned to the bedroom and saw that I'd received a stream of New Year's greeting text messages from my colleagues. I suddenly felt utterly exhausted, so I turned off my mobile, covered my head and fell into a deep sleep. For a while I dreamt about a balloon in the sky smashing its way through the pink clouds. For a while I dreamt that all Ji Lianna's herbs had turned into prickly cacti. For a while I dreamt that water was flooding out the Songhua River, turning Harbin into an island and Ji Lianna and I sat on the roof waiting to be rescued. When Ji Lianna started calling me awake, I was dreaming that I was making sweet-and-sour fillets, and telling Ji Lianna to come and try them. I suddenly looked up at her, but I was still thinking about my cooking, and in bewilderment I asked, 'Do you like the taste?'

'Yes, it's rather nice,' said Ji Lianna. 'It's hard to find decent green tea at this time of year, but these leaves are very fresh. The ginger's pleasant too – the flavour intensifies as you chew it. It's just that dried fruit I'm not sure about.'

I sat up a moment, and remembered where I was. 'That's the betel nut you're talking about. I'm not a huge fan either.'

The reason Ji Lianna was waking me was because it was almost time to go to Modern. Modern was a ten-minute walk from our place, but Ji Lianna had trouble with her legs and feet, added to which it was cold and the road was slippery, so we had to factor in at least twenty minutes to get there. Also, Ji Lianna was very meticulous about her appearance when stepping out. Before going downstairs each day for her coffee, she would make sure she was immaculately dressed, and this was even more so the case when visiting Modern. 'Wash your face, change into your white jumper, and then sit down on the piano stool so I can do your make up,' she instructed. I obeyed, washing my face, changing my clothes, and compliantly sitting down on the piano stool. Ji Lianna carried over her makeup box. First she applied some face cream, followed by a thin layer of powder, before lightly tracing my eyebrows. She dipped a comb into her styling mousse and in a couple of strokes she had combed back my hair. She placed the makeup box on the piano lid and went to fetch the cerise angora scarf. 'There we go . . .' she said, wrapping it loosely around my neck. She told me to look at myself in the mirror while she went to do her own make-up.

To be honest, I didn't believe that a mere seven or eight minutes and such a light layer of makeup would be enough to transform my face. I sat down on the piano stool for a while, before lifting my head and looking into the mirror.

I was completely blown away. I felt as if I was watching the sunrise. I couldn't remember ever having looked this fresh-faced, glossy and beautiful. The scarf Ji Lianna had given me made my unremarkable white jumper look as if it were reflecting countless rays of sunset red, giving it a whole new brilliance. My hairstyle looked sophisticated, while the makeup highlighted my features perfectly, and the sadness in my eyes added a beguiling quality to my face. I stared intently at my reflection and felt my mood gradually lifting.

It turned out that being well made-up really was an effective medicine for perking up the spirits.

Ji Lianna took a long time getting herself ready and it was half an hour before she leisurely walked out. She must have seen her astonishing beauty reflected in my gaze and for a moment I saw the delight flash across her eyes, although the words she spoke were ones of scorn. 'At the end of the day it's impossible to compete with the young. You've got a good base and it only takes three or four minutes for you to look fresh and bright. I need a lot longer, and even then I can't hide the fact that I have an old woman's face!'

Ji Lianna was wearing a full-length black woollen dress with a wide neck, worn slightly off the right shoulder, while close to her left shoulder she'd attached a large crystal brooch shaped like a snowflake, glimmering and glistening as if she'd pinned down a fragment of youth. Usually she wore her hair up, but that day she'd braided it into one loose plait behind her head, tied with dark brown ribbon. She had a thick layer of foundation on her face, which made the wrinkles around her eyes almost invisible. Her lashes had been gently curled, and they were tilted attractively upwards, setting off her eyes, making them appear even brighter and purer, like two pieces of clear watery jade.

I threw my arms around Ji Lianna, and unable to stop myself, blurted, 'Gosh, you're so beautiful . . .'

Ji Lianna patted my back, and in a voice infused with warmth she said, 'All women are beautiful over New Year!'

If you were to describe Central Avenue as Harbin's true self, Modern was its true soul. The hotel was over a hundred years old, and both in the past and now, it was the most fashionable building in the street, demonstrating the point that real style had no reason to fear time. The front of the building was as magnificent as a Chinese landscape painting: the window and overhanging balconies were like a series of overlapping hills, the swirling topaz beneath the balcony platform was like clouds floating among the mountains, the parapet was a sparkling river, while the dome, a gleaming dark green moon. Each time I passed Modern, I'd turn my head for another look, my heart fluttering as if encountering a long-lost lover.

As Ji Lianna and I took our seats in the European restaurant on Modern's ground floor, the sun was losing its glare. Christmas had just passed and the full-length shop windows in Central Avenue opposite us still had their model Santa Clauses and cartoon sledges on display. Normally there weren't many people in this restaurant outside of meal times, but during New Year's, every restaurant in Central Avenue became like a Potala Palace prayer wheel, turning, turning without ceasing.

Ji Lianna had booked the best table in the restaurant, in the southwest corner, next to the full-length window. The rectangular dining table was laid with a snow-white tablecloth and had a narrow-neck vase holding a single red rose. For the main course Ji Lianna ordered *Foie gras* for me and a pepper steak for herself, with salad and pickled cucumber on the side, and a bottle of Italian red wine. She didn't order borscht, saying that the one she made was better. The waiter poured the red wine into tall wine glasses and Ji Lianna gave it a sniff and offered it the sincere praise, 'Such an intimate smell . . .'

We let the wine breathe for a moment before raising our glasses and drinking to the New Year. After half a glass of wine had hit her stomach, Ji Lianna's face became increasingly animated. She pointed to the Huamei European Restaurant across the street and told me that like Modern, Huamei's founder was also Jewish. The Huamei European Restaurant used to be called Maers Tea and Ji Lianna used to go there when she was little to buy confectionary. She told me that there had been a confectioner named Mr Wu and the sweets he made had been refreshing and flavourful while the fudge was soft and sweet and just slid down your throat. Such a shame this craft had been lost. During the

Cultural Revolution, Huamei's name was changed to The Anti-Revisionist Restaurant. 'And this is an anti-revisionist nose!' she said, pointing at her nose. We both laughed. She had warm recollections of Huamei, but she preferred Modern, she told me. She'd danced here when she was young, when the dance hall was magnificent and grand, superior to the one in New World even, which had been so prominent back then. As she spoke, her eyes softened. I knew something of the history of this restaurant, that its founding owner, Iosif Kaspe, had a son, Semen Kaspe, who studied piano at the Paris Conservatory of Music. He came to Harbin during his summer holidays of 1933 to see his father, but during that time he was kidnapped. His kidnapper sliced his ear off before eventually killing him. When I mentioned this incident to Ji Lianna, her mood slumped straight away. She told me her mother had known Iosif. His son's death had broken his heart and he'd ended up leaving the city, which had both earned him his first pot of gold and brought him incomparable pain and sadness.

I really wanted to ask her who she'd danced with all those years ago, but something told me that asking about her dance partner would be akin to asking her about her love and sorrow, which I knew not to do.

By the time we'd been brought our main course, the light outside had faded and the restaurant's crystal chandeliers lit up. Ji Lianna finished her steak, and wiping her mouth with her napkin, she asked me why I hadn't been in touch with my boyfriend lately. I didn't evade the question, I told her how I'd discovered a box of condoms and a shroud inside Qi Deming's suitcase.

'He travels with a shroud?' Ji Lianna asked with incredulity, her eyes widening.

I nodded and explained that ever since I'd seen the shroud, I'd been having constant nightmares.

Ji Lianna looked at me pityingly and raised her wine glass to meet mine. 'Decent men don't give girls nightmares,' she told me quietly as our glasses clinked.

That was her judgement on my relationship with Qi Deming.

It was completely dark by the time we returned home from Modern. Ji Lianna washed her face and removed her makeup, her old face reappearing, looking utterly worn out. She still did her evening prayer as usual. As I was taking off the cerise scarf with a fair amount of regret, my mobile beeped. It was a text from Qi Deming: *Was that you buying flowers this morning? Was that you carrying a package in the cold wind and crying? Going to a European restaurant to eat with an old foreign woman? If it was you, please respond!*

Even though I was weeping with joy, the message I texted back was brutal: *Are you following me, you lowlife?*

I'm following the path of love and virtue, he replied straight away.

The row of characters appeared in front of my eyes, just like a New Year's olive branch.

8

Just as Qi Deming and I were getting back together, Huang Weina and her husband were splitting up.

Huang Weina's husband, Lin Xu, was a brain surgeon at Harbin Medical University Hospital. He was very tall, with a rectangular face, thick eyebrows, penetrating eyes and soft lips – a combination of hardness and softness that made him look like someone extremely talented. Not long after starting my job at the newspaper, I suffered a spell of very painful migraines. I visited two hospitals, but no one could figure out what was wrong, so Huang Weina arranged for me to see her husband. It was very strange. No sooner had I stepped inside that hospital and shaken Dr Lin's hand that my headache melted away. I joked to Huang Weina about her husband having analgesic hands and how she better keep an eye on him or a patient would steal him away. Sounding sweet but firm, Huang Weina said, 'Bad luck for them. Those paws of his are only ever going to ravish one person . . . and that's me.' Huang Weina's conceit was not unfounded: during her university years she'd been outstandingly beautiful with many admirers, of whom Lin Xu was the Prince Charming she had picked out of the crowd.

But this Prince Charming had not been willing to ride only in her plains; he'd stepped out into a new patch of emerald grass. He'd fallen in love with a patient, a girl eleven years his junior, an art student who studied painting and suffered from mild epilepsy.

Huang Weina was unable to make sense of it. Lin Xu had an attractive, charming wife and a clever, sweet-natured son – why on earth would he go for such an average-looking patient? When Huang Weina received the photos of her husband with this girl, snapped on the sly by the private investigator she'd hired, she was livid. She vented her frustration to me down the phone saying, 'She's even less attractive than you. She's like a scrawny stray cat. Lin Xu's clearly lost his mind!'

This lack of self-censorship was part of Huang Weina's charm, and hearing her comment about the girl being even less attractive than me, I snorted with laughter down the phone and said, 'Thanks for the compliment . . .'

Sounding husky and fatigued, Huang Weina said, 'Zhao Xiao'e, I'm in agony. In hell. And all you have to say to me are quirky things like this!'

It was noon when I knocked on Huang Weina's door. She opened it with blurry eyes, wearing nothing but a purple silk nightdress. As soon as I sat down, she whipped off her nightdress. Leaning forward, slightly and her hands resting casually on her hips in a catwalk model pose, she said, 'Zhao Xiao'e, is this body not good enough?'

I'm being completely and utterly honest when I say that even with all those trips I'd made to the public baths in which I'd seen my fair share of naked women, I'd never seen a body that had come close to perfection. But Huang Weina's was something else. The moment she removed her nightdress, the dimly lit living room brightened. Huang Weina was like a candlestick, radiant and shining.

'Knowing that such perfect bodies exist in the world makes mine seem utterly defective.' I sighed in dismay. 'No wonder I'm having such an issue getting married. Dr Lin really has no idea how good he has it.'

'And this is after giving birth.' Huang Weina stopped flaunting herself, put her nightdress back on and lit up a cigarette. Not without some pride she said, 'My body was even better when I was younger! I'm not trying to insult Lin Xu here, but the first time he was with me, he was inside for less than three minutes before he exploded. That's how hot my body was – it made him detonate instantly!'

Huang Weina laughed with abandon and flung the set of photos at me. These pictures charted Lin Xu's infidelity. 'Look at that beast!' she exclaimed. 'He told me he'd been on nightshift when actually he'd been shacking up with this young hussy. Tell me, in what way is she better than me?'

The girl in the photos looked extremely frail. She had small eyes, a small nose, a crescent mouth and long pitch-black hair that fell naturally around her shoulders. You wouldn't describe her as pretty, but there was something about her that it was hard to put your finger on, something captivating. I didn't dare say this to Huang Weina though.

'What are you planning to do?' I asked.

'Lin Xu has brought up getting a divorce. He says he'd be willing to leave me the house and all its possessions, as long as he can have our son. He must be dreaming! How could he think I'd let our son go and live with that mule! What if she has one of her epileptic fits and throttles him to death?' Huang Weina extinguished the half-smoked cigarette and started coughing.

'Generally when men get divorced, they don't ask for the child,' I said. 'The fact that Lin Xu wants to take Lin Lin shows he's a responsible dad.'

Lin Lin was Huang Weina and Lin Xu's treasured little boy. He'd just started primary school and was shorter than most children his age, a miniature person. He was smart and cheeky and had a slight speech impediment. When he called me Xiao'e, it came out as Sha-shar, which always amused me.

'His little hussy is an invalid – she's not suited to bringing up a child. The only reason they want Lin Lin is to take away my creation! Or, the other possibility, they don't really want him and are only saying it to appear virtuous. If I actually gave in and agreed to let them take him, I bet they'd find some excuse not to. I've heard plenty of cases like that!' Extremely agitated, Huang Weina lit another cigarette.

'The fact that Dr Lin hasn't asked for the house or the car and has said he's prepared to leave you all his possessions must show that he still cares about you,' I said.

'That's just his guilty conscience talking!' Huang Weina took a fierce drag from her cigarette. 'And anyway, he's the central pillar of surgery at that hospital! You know the first violin in the orchestra? Aside from the conductor, it's the most important position in the orchestra. In that hospital, Lin Xu is first knife. That's the equivalent. He's the chief surgeon of at least two operations a day. And it's not simple stuff like cutting out someone's tonsils or appendix – we're talking brain surgery. The patient's family members hand him red envelopes stuffed with cash. I'll be completely open with you, four or five hundred is standard for what you find in red envelopes for a straightforward operation, but for brain surgery the family members are all on tenterhooks and tend to give the chief surgeon six or seven thousand. The hospital's brain surgery department flourishes because of him and our family prospers because of him as well. Without Lin Xu's red envelopes, how would we have been able to afford this house and this car? He might leave all the property and possessions to me in the divorce, but his skill means that he'll be back on his feet in three or four years max, and I'm not going to just stand there submissively and let his little hussy get his golden hands.'

So, in essence, this house had been paid for through the blood of patients . . . As this thought came to me, I had a sudden image of pus and blood filling the room, a red light started flashing in front of my eyes and my nostrils became oddly itchy. My gastric juices started surging and I began to retch.

In Huang Weina's state of fury, she failed to notice my discomfort. She told me that, even if they were getting a divorce, she wasn't going to let Lin Xu off the hook that easily. She was going to destroy their new living set-up. 'In the eyes of the law he's still my husband. I know where they shack up together and when he doesn't return home at night and he isn't on night shift, that's where I'll go, demanding they let me sleep there with them. And if they don't open the door to me, I'll start beating a gong! Back in the day, my father used to beat a gong in the rural Yangge opera troupe, and he left me a huge copper gong when he died, which I'm planning to put to good use!' Her plan was to exhaust them both mentally and physically, destroy their reputations and cause them such feelings of self-disgust that they'd just give up on the relationship in the end. Once he'd had his change of heart and come back to her, she'd kick him to the curb.

'Since you'll be getting a divorce either way, why not just let him go now?' I asked.

'Because it would make it far too easy for them,' explained Huang Weina.

I'd always thought of Huang Weina as such an independent, generous and laidback woman. I'd had no idea that she could be so selfish and narrow-minded. It seemed that as soon as men and woman fell out, they stopped being emotional animals and turned into objects; as emotions you couldn't set a price on, while objects could be bought and sold.

Once Huang Weina had finished her rant, she appeared a lot calmer. She asked me whether I'd met anyone recently. I nodded and asked how she could tell. 'What else brings that tender look to a girl's eyes other than a few sweet words from some scumbag man!' she commented with disdain. 'But just you remember, sooner or later that sweetness disappears. Remind yourself how Song Xiangkui treated you and how Lin Xu treated me. Clever women never give themselves to a man. Women are the roses and men are the bees. Once he's sucked out all your nectar and you no longer taste sweet, he'll fly off to the next rose. In this respect, Ji Lianna is the smartest woman I know; she's never in her life truly given herself and never been hurt to the bone.'

I was feeling very close to Qi Deming at the time, which made Huang Weina's words feel particularly intrusive.

'Perhaps Ji Lianna's romantic life isn't the blank sheet of paper we've imagined it to be,' I told her, and went on to explain how during New Year's, when she invited me to Modern, she'd dressed up to look young and beautiful for our meal and told me she'd danced there when she was young.

'Dancing? Why didn't she mention this during the interview?' Huang Weina was stumped for a moment, before saying, 'perhaps that's the day she returns to think back over the memories of her old lover?'

'There's no doubt in my mind that Ji Lianna had experienced a love that has been engraved on her soul,' I said.

Huang Weina gave a snort and blew a smoke ring into my face. 'Silly little girl,' she said dismissively. 'It was probably unrequited love! If she'd actually experienced it, it wouldn't be engraved on her soul.'

Spring Festival was just around the corner. No one at the newspaper liked to be on the rota over Spring Festival. But for a person like me, without parents to run back and see, working overtime over Spring Festival was actually a good thing. Finding yourself alone at the moment the night sky was being lit up by fireworks made you feel completely detached from all that was wonderful in the world, it left you feeling abandoned and magnified the bleakness. Working in the office over Spring Festival made the festivities much easier to handle. My boss had picked up on how I'd volunteer myself to be put on the Spring Festival rota each year and made a point of granting me a week off before the festivities.

On the last day of the lunar year, I made a quick trip to Keshan to visit my mother's grave, as it was our local custom to do on that date. My brother accompanied me to the Western Hills cemetery and on the way there we saw Old Yang from the clinic, our stepmother's former lover. He was dressed in ragged clothes, carrying a shovel and loitering in the entrance to the village, looking like a ghost. When he saw us he said, 'Be kind and bury me! There is no sunshine in this world and I'm afraid of the dark. Please, just go ahead and bury me.'

My brother told me the tale of Old Yang's misfortune. Two years ago, his son had died after a sudden cerebral infarction, and that very same year his son's widow remarried. Meanwhile in a state of devastation, his divorced daughter turned to drugs and was sent to a rehabilitation centre. Overnight, all his grandchildren had lost their homes and Old Yang became responsible for them all. And if that wasn't bad enough, at that time there was an issue with Old Yang's medical clinic too: following his week-long course of muscular acupuncture with Old Yang, an eight-year-old boy had suddenly discovered that he lost proper function in his leg. This boy's family took him to the provincial capital hospital to be seen by a doctor, where diagnostic tests showed that the disability had been caused by improper use of acupuncture. A medical malpractice case ensued, which resulted in the revoking of Old Yang's medical licence.

Terrified of prison, he sold his property and withdrew all his funds to try and settle privately with the family, but it wasn't enough for the compensation, and he still had a debt of over 10 000 *yuan*. The pressure caused Old Yang to go crazy and now he always carried a shovel with him and begged passersby to bury him. My brother told me that things hadn't been good for our stepmother over the last two years either. That autumn she'd been shameless to go and see her old lover, not expecting to bump into him in his crazy state before she'd even entered the village. Old Yang's white beard floated about as he fixed his eyes on her and walked over with the shovel in his hand saying, 'Young lady, please have a heart and bury me! If you do, it will bring you good luck. Every cob of corn in your field will grow into a gold bar!' A villager who had witnessed this scene reported back about how stupefied stepmother was. She'd given a long sigh, turned around and left, without even setting foot in the village.

Knowing that my stepmother and her lover had got their comeuppances filled me with delight, even though I knew that this was a warped reaction to have. It was with this sense of glee that I returned to Harbin, feeling energised. As Qi Deming took me in his arms, I felt filled with a fiery passion. 'Why have you come back from your hometown so sweet?' Qi Deming joked.

'They grow so much beet in my home town that going back there is like bathing in a jar of honey. It sweetens everyone!'

9

Qi Deming went to spend Spring Festival at his father's, while I worked my shift at the newspaper office.

Ji Lianna had got into the habit of spending Spring Festival on her own. On the eve of Chinese New Year she didn't eat dumplings or anything like that; instead she had a pot of tea and a dish of dried fruit while she played a piece on the piano – her own Chinese New Year's ritual. I asked her what song she usually played at this time – Chopin, Mozart or Schumann? Ji Lianna gave a quiet laugh and said, 'I play whatever my fingertips lead me to play.' Ji Lianna was profoundly knowledgeable about the piano and revered the Jewish pianist, Vladimir Horowitz. After retiring from her job teaching music at the school, she had started giving piano lessons privately. Later, when she became older, she told me she only played for *Him*, and no longer as a source of income.

In the south, Chinese folklore depicted the Spring Festival beast as a bear coming out of hibernation. As soon as he emerged from his cave, spring was said to have arrived. But in the North, the Spring Festival beast was a snow rabbit bounding over the vast plains. But Spring Festival actually arrived too early for this rabbit, at the time of Chinese New Year, it was still too cold for his white fur to have turned brown and be ruffled by the spring breeze.

I imagined that Huang Weina and Doctor Lin's separation would have meant a miserable Spring Festival for her, but one week after Spring Festival, she arrived back at work looking radiant. She'd taken her son skiing at Yabuli for the holidays, she said. Oh, kids picked things up so fast; Lin Lin had learned to ski in three days, apparently.

'Did Dr Lin go with you?' I asked.

'Of course! We wouldn't have been able to go without him.' she said jovially. 'I'd have had to spend Spring Festival banging my gong in their doorway!'

I assumed this meant they'd reconciled and the threat had passed.

Huang Weina told me that while in Yabuli, she'd interviewed the descendant of a wealthy Jewish merchant. She'd mentioned Ji Lianna's name to him and found out that my landlady's stepfather had shared close ties with the Japanese who'd been occupying northeast China at the time and that he'd even promised Ji Lianna's hand in marriage to a Japanese officer. Ji Lianna had refused and a period of bad mental health had ensued. So it did indeed seem as if Ji Lianna had a story to tell about her personal life.

'No wonder she behaves so differently with people now,' I said.

I'd read that when the Japanese had occupied northeast China, they'd been secretly promoting something known as the *Fugu Plan,* in which they'd promise to give Jews land so that they could revive the Jewish state. The motive of the Japanese had actually been to suck up all the Jewish capital they could get, in order to invest in the military and industrial construction. Japanese people loved to eat puffer fish, which was toxic but tasted divine. The name *Fugu Plan,* or the *Puffer Fish Programme,* perfectly illustrated the ingenious but risky nature of this plan. To increase the benefits they derived from that north-eastern territory, the Japanese adopted a policy of friendship towards the Jewish people. The kidnapping of Modern's founder's son had involved the Japanese, apparently. The Japanese saw Modern as a succulent piece of meat, which they wanted to buy at a low price. But Iosif Kaspe wasn't prepared to sell to them and astounded them by the high price he quoted for it. Iosif Kaspe knew that by so doing he would enrage the Japanese, and while increasing his own protection and always travelling with bodyguards, he also transferred his property over to his son who had French nationality, and hung a Tricolour flag outside the front of Modern. The Japanese were incensed, but unable to find an opportunity to attack Iosif Kaspe, they ordered bandits to instead abduct his son, who was back visiting his father over the holidays. This led to a tragedy that shocked the world. When Huang Weina spoke of the abduction, she didn't have much good to say about Iosif Kaspe. She told me that when his son was first abducted, the bandits cut off his ear and sent it to him, saying that if he paid ransom, they'd let his son go. But Iosif Kaspe refused to negotiate with them, saying unless he could see his son he wouldn't pay anything. The kidnappers sensed that it was like squeezing water from a stone, and in an act of fury, they murdered the boy. 'If Lin Lin was abducted, forget money, I'd cut off a lump of my own flesh!' Huang Weina said, breathlessly. For this reason, she had a negative view of Modern, referring to it as *The Haunted House*.

Was Ji Lianna's stepfather close to the Japanese because he'd signed up for the *Puffer Fish Programme*? I was fascinated by what kind of Japanese army officer would have taken a liking to a Jewish girl during that time.

The major Jewish festival was called Passover and as ceremonious for them as Spring Festival was for us. Passover fell towards the end of April that year. Harbin's government-controlled central heating had been turned off by then and all those boilers had stopped piping out their exhaust fumes. The air was allowed space to breathe once more and blue skies returned to the city. The grass shot up, spring jasmine and fuschia bloomed, and people filled the streets. Spring was a radiant and lovely time. It offered everything a chance for rebirth and carried us far from the smoke and ash of the winter. A week before Passover Ji Lianna started to prepare for the festival. She hired someone to come in and sweep the place, wash the curtains and bedding, wipe the windows and re-hook the curtains with the new copper hooks. After all of this, the place sparkled like new, and felt fresh and reinvigorated. The day before Passover she bought a lamb bone, which she sprinkled with herbs and roasted in the oven. Next, she made white flour pancakes. During the Passover period, Jews couldn't eat leavened food and she didn't touch Modern's bread for seven days. Ji Lianna explained that she used to spend Passover with old friends, but they were all gone now and she had no one to invite over. 'It's no good living a long time,' she said, sounding disheartened. 'You have to see more death than other people. Why hasn't *He* come to collect me yet?' she muttered over and over.

'*He* has so many disasters in the world to oversee, *He* hasn't had time to deal with you yet,' I said.

'Death isn't a disaster,' Ji Lianna told me sternly. 'It's rebirth. The most joyous aspect of life.'

I hadn't actually said that death was a disaster; Ji Lianna must have misunderstood me. But I got comfort from her misunderstanding, thinking how my reborn mother would no longer have to suffer humiliation. Perhaps she'd been reborn as a bird and was at this very moment flying through some sky I couldn't see. Perhaps she'd turned into a beautiful snake; neither wind nor rain able to dampen her spirit. I only hoped that she hadn't been reborn as a person, as I was scared she would suffer more mortal-world bitterness.

At the end of April, Qi Deming took his shroud and went off on another business trip to promote new drugs, this time to Jiangxi. He was away from Harbin throughout the whole Passover period, so Ji Lianna and I spent it together.

On the morning of Passover, Ji Lianna mashed up rhododendrons and hydrangeas to make a red paste, a symbolic alternative to lamb's blood, which she smeared over her doorframe. This custom came from a Biblical story. The Israelites had been enslaved in Egypt and wanted to escape their misery, but the Egyptian Pharaoh refused to let them go. Through the prophet Moses, God sent down a number of different disasters: a plague of locusts, a plague of livestock, of flies, darkness and so on. The Egyptians suffered these cruel disasters, but still the Pharaoh refused to let the Israelites go. So, God cast down his tenth plague, to kill all the first-borns in Egypt, man and beast. To stop the Israelites from being killed, God told Moses to instruct all Israelite families to slaughter a lamb and smear its blood on the doorframe. God would see the houses with lamb blood on their doorframes and simply *pass over* them, keeping the Israelites safe. The Israelites escaped from Egypt in such haste that the bread they took with them hadn't had the chance to rise and to commemorate this, Jewish people dined on a bone of lamb eaten with unleavened bread.

Ji Lianna prepared a lavish Passover dinner and then called Huang Weina to invite her over to join us. Huang Weina asked if she could bring her son. '*He* loves children, please do,' Ji Lianna said.

Huang Weina had been extremely thoughtful, bringing Ji Lianna a box of almond biscuits, a tin of Italian coffee and a couple of branches of pale yellow spring jasmine. I asked her where she'd got the flowers. Bold as brass she said, 'Well, seeing as the florist doesn't sell spring jasmine, you can probably deduce that I stole it! But stealing flowers is like stealing books, it doesn't count as stealing!' She finished with a proud little laugh.

The spring jasmine had exploded into bloom in the little garden beneath our office, but none of the workers hurrying to and fro on their nine to five schedules, had time to appreciate the flowers. The way Huang Weina saw it, blossoming in a place like that was lonely for the flowers. They would far rather be plucked and given to someone who cherished their beauty, and to blossom in appreciative company. I'd also given Ji Lianna some flowers, and although mine were florist-bought, they were still rather special. I'd asked the florist to use rattan to weave a Star of David, studding it with small yellow roses, adorned with silvery-white baby's breath. Ji Lianna absolutely adored the composition, whose fragrance pervaded the whole place and she'd carried the bright and beautiful object into her prayer room as an offering to *Him*.

Ji Lianna usually ate stooped over the small table next to the piano, but this table was too small to use when there were guests, so she brought the folding white oak table through from the kitchen. No one had spent Passover with her since her old friends had passed away and this folding table hadn't been used for years, a thought that left me a little cold. But as soon as Ji Lianna had dusted the table, spread it with a white tablecloth with a pink flower pattern, and placed a square pottery vase arranged with the spring jasmine in the centre, it was transformed, giving off the jubilant air of spring. Ji Lianna stared at the spring jasmine, appearing to get lost in thought. She gave a deep sigh and said that the blossom was absolutely exquisite. It reminded her a lot of the Japanese allspice she'd seen in Suzhou. The only thing that this jasmine lacked was the delicate fragrance of the allspice.

Huang Weina immediately followed this up with the question, 'What year did you go to Suzhou?'

'Sixty-one years ago . . . ' Ji Lianna said, sounding sad.

'With your parents?' Huang Weina cut in.

'On my own,' Ji Lianna said. 'I wanted to go and see the flowers on my own.'

The flowers started to make Huang Weina nostalgic too. 'When my father was in the late stages of his cancer, he was very keen to go and see the peonies, so I went with him to Heze. After three days of looking at peonies, he said he was ready to go home. On the plane home he took my hand and told me the peony was the courtesan of the flowers, but even the brightest and most beautiful flowers flourished and then wilted, and the same would be true of him. Before that, he'd been afraid of death, but after seeing the peonies he no longer was. I was grateful to the peonies for allowing him to go peacefully.'

I didn't want to let Huang Weina slip into a melancholic state during Passover so I bustled her and Lin Lin out to the balcony to fetch a folding chair, while I helped Ji Lianna carry the food out from the kitchen and lay it on the table.

The dining table had been placed in the centre of the living room and right below the stained glass Star of David lamp. Colourful patterns were reflected down onto the table, shining down onto the vegetables and the lamb bone, making it all look dazzling. Before sitting down, Ji Lianna went off to pray and then instructed us all to wash our hands. The Passover evening meal had begun. First, we drank a glass of red wine. Next, we ate vegetables marinated in brine, boiled eggs with their shells removed, unleavened bread and the lamb bone. Ji Lianna had even gone to the trouble of squeezing Lin Lin a pear juice and making him apple pie. After three glasses of wine, Ji Lianna told Lin Lin the Passover story. When she got to the part about Moses leading the Israelites out of Egypt, how he'd lifted his staff and parted the Red Sea, creating a road for the Israelites to cross it, while the pursuing Pharaoh of Egypt's army all drowned, Lin Lin's eyes opened wide in amazement. 'Who's Moses?' he asked. 'How come he has such a badass staff? Is it as badass as the Monkey King's golden cudgel?'

Huang Weina scolded Lin Lin for his bad language, but Ji Lianna said she didn't mind. 'Moses is the Lord,' she explained, giving him some apple pie.

'Is he still alive?' asked Lin Lin.

'The Lord can't die,' replied Ji Lianna.

To which Lin Lin asked, 'Have you ever seen him?'

Ji Lianna gave a slight shake of the head. 'Every day I wait for him to come,' she said softly.

'If Moses can't ever die, I guess his hair must have gone white a long time ago and he probably finds it difficult to walk,' Lin Lin said with empathy. 'It's probably hard to see him if he doesn't get around too well.'

Huang Weina had just taken a sip of red wine and hearing Lin Lin say this, she laughed so much it spurted out her mouth, splashing all over me and turning my white jumper plum red. We drank a fair amount that evening and Ji Lianna told many stories about other Jewish festivals, such as Pentecost and the Feast of Tabernacles. She told us that before, families used to build huts on the banks of the Songhua River out of willow branches to celebrate Tabernacle. Each family would take the Hebrew Bible and plenty of fruit and live in the hut for a week. Tabernacle usually fell in October, often at the beginning of the month when the sun still shone brightly, but sometimes it fell at the end of the month when the snowflakes had started to fall. According to the scriptures, during the seven days of Tabernacle, seven heroes would visit the hut, one each day, but on the days that it was bitterly cold, the women and children were allowed to go back home and the man of the household would stay in the hut on his own to greet those heroes. Lin Lin asked if Monkey King was among these seven heroes, and we all shook our heads. Lin Lin was disappointed about this. He announced that he was full, got down from the table and went to the balcony to look at the view.

When Ji Lianna drank alcohol, she didn't appear drunk and continued to be very sharp. Several times Huang Weina tried to bring the conversation round to the old lady's private life, but each time she was met with soft but firm resistance. An example of this was when Huang Weina asked her what district of Harbin the Japanese used to live in. This area, Ji Lianna said plainly. Next, Huang Weina asked her what the universal standard for an attractive man had been back then. Ji Lianna gave Huang Weina a sympathetic look and told her that the man you fell in love with was the one you found attractive and how there couldn't possibly be a universal standard for this. Then, Huang Weina asked whether a woman like her, who'd never married, had been looked down upon at all back then. 'As long as you don't look down upon yourself, who cares what the rest of the world thinks?' was Ji Lianna's eloquent reply. Huang Weina and I started to think about the fate of those fleeing Jews. We exchanged a hopeless look, knowing that the evening was drawing to a close.

As Huang Weina was leaving, she seemed a bit despondent. As I escorted her and Lin Lin down the stairs, she gave a sigh and said, 'Sitting opposite a living legend and not being allowed to turn the pages. That's really hard!'

'She's the author of the legend. She has a right to keep it to herself,' I said.

I had grown to like Ji Lianna more, the more I knew her.

The night before the May Day holiday, Qi Deming was due to come back. Before taking off from Wenzhou airport, he called me and said he hoped he might find me waiting for him at the Zhongshan Gardens apartment when he got back.

'Is it me you want waiting for you, or a home-cooked meal?' I teased.

Qi Deming laughed and said, 'Oh, how well you know me!'

Thinking of the shroud in his suitcase, I made a point of wishing him a safe journey.

While I was in Carrefour buying ingredients for our reunion dinner, I looked up and saw Song Xiangkui standing in front of the freezer section. His chin was covered in stubble, his face was sallow and he'd lost a lot of weight. When he saw me, the hand he was holding the shopping basket with started to tremble slightly. I noticed dates, a box of strawberries and a whole frozen chicken in his basket. We were both a bit embarrassed and avoided each other's gaze, not sure quite how to greet each other. I was the one to eventually break the silence. 'So you're here doing your shopping then?'

'Yep, shopping,' he replied.

'How's Liu Qin doing?' I asked.

After a pause he said, 'She's pregnant.'

'Congratulations, father-to-be!' I said.

With a distinct lack of joy in his eyes Song Xiangkui said, 'I've been meaning to call you for a while, as it happens. I wanted to talk to you, Xiao'e. What a coincidence to run into you today. Do you have half an hour? I could wait for you in the Pizza Hut downstairs and we could have a coffee together.'

I looked at my watch. 'I don't have time today, I'm afraid. My boyfriend's getting back from a trip out of town. His plane is about to land and I'm in a bit of a hurry as I'm cooking for him.'

'Ah, that's the reason you're looking so attractive,' Song Xiangkui said sorrowfully. 'I should have known you'd have a boyfriend.' Muttering an apology, he bid me a hurried farewell.

It was dark by the time I got to Qi Deming's. I'd just finished cooking when the phone rang. Qi Deming told me he'd landed, but had managed to hit rush hour, there was a lot of congestion entering the city and he estimated it would take about fifty minutes to get back. He told me not to be worried about his delay. As I was mopping the floor, I thought about Song Xiangkui's gaunt face and started to feel worried about him. I put down the mop and sent him a text message asking: *Is it a good time to speak?* Song Xiangkui phoned me straight away, explaining that he was in a hotel on his own. I asked what he'd wanted to talk to me about. He told me he and his mother were worried out of their minds that his and Liu Qin's child could be born congenitally deaf. He'd consulted with the doctor and found out that a child born to a congenitally deaf woman and a hearing man could well turn out to be deaf. Song Xiangkui moaned about how he always had the worst luck, never once had he won even the five-*yuan* prizes when he bought a lottery ticket. If he ended up in a family with two deaf people, one crazy one, plus his disabled and unmarriable brother, he was sure to go crazy, too. He wanted Liu Qin to terminate the pregnancy, but she was determined to keep the child. Song Xiangkui told me he took sleeping pills every night, but still couldn't sleep. He missed the days we'd shared, he said, he even missed our rows – it had all turned to beautiful memories.

Song Xiangkui's nostalgia gave me the courage to come out with the question I'd been storing up this whole time. 'Please be straight with me. When you broke up with me, did it have anything to do with Liu Qin's house?'

I knew that asking such a question at a time like this was the same as delivering him a slap across the face. Song Xiangkui was silent a moment before roaring, 'Zhao Xiao'e!

People like us who come from the countryside and have no background, no money and no defining abilities, really shouldn't have chosen the big city to make our home! Why are we living and working so hard, tiring ourselves out so!'

Song Xiangkui cursed as he hung up the phone. Indirectly, he had indeed answered my question. I sat there blankly for a while, weighing it all up, before sending him a comforting text message: *Don't worry too much about whether your child is deaf or not. Every child is an angel sent from God! As long as you are happy in yourself, you can have a happy life, even in a world without words or sound.* I knew that my words sounded flippant and empty and Song Xiangkui didn't reply – of course he didn't.

As soon as Qi Deming came back that evening, he washed his face before hurriedly opening his suitcase saying, 'Look, Zhao Xiao'e, you'll be so proud of me. You were on my mind so much that I didn't need any of the condoms I took with me.'

'I wasn't scared of you using the condoms, I was scared of you using the shroud,' I replied.

'Oh, Xiao'e!' Qi Deming said, his voice trembling.

He hugged me tightly to him and cried. After Wang Ke, he was the second man I'd held in my arms while he'd dampened me with his tears.

1 0

On the last day of the Labour Day holidays, Qi Deming invited me to meet his father. I felt euphoric; it was a sign he was actually serious about me and perhaps might be about to propose. His father suggested we meet at his printing factory in Daowai district. Qi Deming said his father might have been concerned I'd be nervous and thought the lively atmosphere of the workshop would help keep things relaxed. But the way I saw it, the style of meeting he'd proposed displayed something of his indifference about his son's romantic life.

The meeting was scheduled for 2 p.m., but I started to get ready after breakfast. I went through all my spring clothes, trying them on item by item. Most of them from the market and poor quality, making it difficult for me to dress strikingly. I tried to randomly match different items together, turning left and then right in front of the mirror, but nothing said yes, and I started getting upset. Ji Lianna saw me fretting and, realising that I had an important engagement, came over to help. Who was I meeting, she asked. I asked her what difference it made; I simply wanted to make myself look pretty. Of course, it made a difference, Ji Lianna said. If I were meeting work friends, she'd advise me to dress smart-casual, and for such an occasion my cream double-breasted trench coat with my long dark brown scarf would be ideal. If it was my boyfriend I was meeting, during this wonderful spring weather, she would suggest something vivid and a little risqué, those mauve cropped trousers paired with my wide-neck, off-the-shoulder purple patterned jumper perhaps, a little like a lilac bush. If I were meeting distinguished elders, meanwhile, I should dress somewhat more conservatively, in my blue and white checked jacket with my long black skirt, perhaps. I was meeting Qi Deming's father, I told Ji Lianna.

'Oh,' Ji Lianna said, her mood slumping. 'Are you going to his house?' she asked indifferently.

'We're meeting at the workshop of his Daowai printing factory,' I explained. Ji Lianna looked aghast. 'And you agreed?'

I nodded.

Ji Lianna hung her head in disappointment and said, 'Wear your cream trench coat with your black trousers, in that case. Treat it like a stroll along the Songhua River. Wear your knitted turtleneck under the coat and so you won't need a scarf. You shouldn't wear scarves in those sorts of places, they might get caught up in the machines and strangle you.'

Ji Lianna's warning reminded me of the fate of the American modern dance choreographer, Isadora Duncan, who was killed by her scarf. She'd been out taking a ride in a racing car, with a thick red scarf wrapped around her neck. One end of the scarf was flowing out behind her, and just happened to drop down beneath the back wheel. As soon as the car started, Isadora got dragged out of the racing car by the trapped scarf. By the time the driver realised and applied the brakes, Isadora's struggle was over. There was no way she could have imagined that soft silk garment might act as her killer. Isadora's end was a stunning modern dance performance. I didn't think that would be my fate. The way I saw it, such a romantic tragedies were reserved for artists.

I had faith in Ji Lianna's vision and intuition, and dressed exactly as she'd advised. The resulting outfit was becoming, stylish but natural. If you wear a trench coat, you can walk outside at any time, even if it's windy or raining, Ji Lianna added pointedly.

There was still some time before the meeting, and I decided to go out and walk around, try and drum up some courage.

The way I saw it, living alone for such a long time meant that Ji Lianna was obviously very brave. Time and time again I wondered where Ji Lianna's courage for survival came from? Was it from that romantic love she'd never forgotten, or from the comfort of religion? I was more inclined to believe it was from the latter, because the former was like mist or smoke to me, leaving no clear picture, while the latter I witnessed every day in the form of her pious chanting and it had left a deep impression.

I decided to go and take a wander around the synagogue, thinking it must be the place Ji Lianna derived her courage.

There were two synagogues in Harbin, both in Daoli district, not far away. The old Jewish synagogue was on

Tongjiang Street, previously called Artillery Street and inaugurated in 1909. It was Harbin's early centre of Jewish religious activity. In 1931 there was a fire in the old synagogue and after being repaired and expanded, the ground floor still served as a synagogue, while the first and second floors housed Harbin's Jewish religious and cultural administrative bodies, including the Jewish Religious Association, the Jewish Zionist Organization, the Jewish Funeral Society, the *Jewish Life* editorial department and so on. From the side, the old synagogue looked a lot like an early cruise ship. On top of its red brick hemispherical dome a silver Star of David stood like a lighthouse. This cruise ship had been travelling for a century, but still hadn't reached its destination, showing you that religion travelled across boundless shores. Nowadays the old synagogue housed a youth hostel, with its first and second floors converted into guest rooms for travellers who were nostalgic about the past. The ground floor featured a quaint little café, attracting those who sought out new experiences.

The new Jewish synagogue was located at the crossroads between Jingwei Street and Anguo Street and was inaugurated in 1921. It was a solid, but attractive building, red and white mainly, with a golden double-centre dome that looked like a big ripe pumpkin. The synagogue had held seven or eight hundred people and as well as being used for worship, it was also where wedding ceremonies were conducted. Ji Lianna said that bitter cries often used to resound from the synagogue during worship. She didn't need to explain; I understood the reason for this crying. Freezing cold Harbin had become a refuge for these Jewish people, but it wasn't their home.

Ji Lianna seemed to have a deeper attachment to the New Jewish synagogue. She told me that was where her mother and stepfather had married. At Tabernacle each year, everyone living in huts along the banks of the Songhua River would come to the New Synagogue to pray. This synagogue had been damaged during the Cultural Revolution and after it was repaired, it was turned into Eastern Entertainment City, a swanky nightclub, the flowing wine and bright lights wiping out the tears of the Jewish people. Later the city government rebuilt the synagogue in accordance to its original appearance and opened a museum dedicated to the history and culture of the Jewish people. Although the rebuilding project of the New Synagogue hadn't been as good as Ji Lianna had been hoping, she was still overjoyed at its rebirth.

The New Synagogue wasn't far from Ji Lianna's and even though it was hemmed in by modern high-rise buildings, with no shade offered by trees, right in the centre of the transportation hub and plagued by car exhaust fumes, it was still the most fascinating building in the area. True beauty seemed to keep itself secluded from the world.

Even though it was a national holiday, the New Synagogue's ticket counter was completely deserted and I bought myself a ticket without having to queue. Perhaps because of the bad things I'd said to Ji Lianna about *Him*, as soon as I stepped into the hall, I started to feel slightly afraid.

I'd only just started looking around at the synagogue when my mobile phone started to ring in my bag. It was Qi Deming calling to tell me his father wanted us to meet at eleven instead. He asked if I could quickly get myself ready and he'd pick me up on the way.

'Is your dad always this flaky?' I asked, slightly peeved.

'He changed the time because he wants to take us out for lunch,' Qi Deming said sounding elated. 'I'll have you know that he's never taken a friend of mine out for a meal before.'

'I'm not keen on sudden changes of plan,' I muttered, thinking how lucky it was that I'd got myself ready ahead of time.

'You sound like you're out and about? Are you tied up with something?' Qi Deming asked anxiously.

I looked at my watch, half past nine. It wouldn't take more than half an hour to get from here to Daowai, even with traffic. 'I've just arrived at the synagogue,' I told him. 'You can come and pick me up from here. Just give me a buzz when you're nearby.'

'Are you there with Ji Lianna?' Qi Deming asked.

'No, on my own,' I said.

'There are two synagogues, are you at the one with the red roof or the one with the golden roof?' I was surprised by how familiar Qi Deming sounded with these two synagogues.

'The one with the golden domed roof on Jingwei Street,' I said.

'Ah, the Entertainment City one,' Qi Deming said. 'I'm going outside to hail a taxi now. I'll be with you in around twenty minutes.'

Outside it had really felt like spring had arrived, but inside the synagogue it was extremely cool, and feeling a chill, I couldn't hold back a sneeze. There was a huge Star of David mosaic in the centre of the hall's marble floor. I walked towards it, hoping it would bring me warmth. Soon I realised with disappointment, that it wasn't starlight seeping out from under my feet, but the brilliant light cast down by a crystal chandelier. The new synagogue's reconstruction seemed to have left it looking too modern, lacking the solemn grandeur I'd been expecting. On the wall in front hung a huge black and white photograph, just like a dark window giving me a glimpse into the local Jewish past. The photograph depicted a grand gathering of gentlemen at Modern. I stared at the men in the photo, scrutinising each in turn and discovering that although they all looked very different, they all gave off the sense that they had a story to tell. They seemed worlds apart from contemporary men, whose expressions in photographs were never as intriguing.

Ji Lianna had told me that there was a beautiful brass seven-stick candelabra that I could see in the new synagogue exhibition space, which had been donated by her friend. I stepped out of the Star of David and went upstairs in search of the candelabra. On the way there, I suddenly remembered the meeting with Qi Deming's father and that it was customary for young people to bring fruit or some other token gift when meeting with members of the older generation.

When I called Qi Deming to ask him about this, he was already in a cab. 'There's no need to bring anything. He has everything he needs. And anyway, you're not going to his house or even his office. He's being casual, so we can follow suit!'

I had lost interest in seeing the candelabra and decided to leave the synagogue early to wait for him. I'd been waiting a quarter of an hour when Qi Deming gave me a buzz. He'd hailed a red Xiali hatchback, and before I could even see the car, I could hear its music. 'Zhao Xiao'e . . .' he shouted, poking his head out the window. The way he called my name made me feel as if we were flesh and blood. My whole body flooded with warmth and I felt myself start to relax.

Qi Deming had been sitting in the front, but as soon as the taxi came to a stop, he popped out, opened the back door and sat down in there next to me. As he was doubling over to get inside, he patted me on the behind and said, 'Very nice costume you have on today. You're looking stylish!' It may have been a compliment, but the word costume made me think of drama, which gave me a bad feeling.

I asked Qi Deming how he knew both the synagogues so well. He explained that he'd lived in this area when he was younger. The New Synagogue had been the Entertainment City back then, and very lively, until they turned it into a museum, after which it became quiet. He liked the youth hostel in the old synagogue, which he'd stayed at once, and found its little restaurant very atmospheric. 'If I ever propose to you, that's where I'll do it!' he said with a wink.

Considering the fact that he'd always lived in Harbin, there was only reason I could think of why he'd spent the night in a youth hostel and that was to get a room with a girl. Filled with jealousy I said, 'If you ever take another little hussy to stay there, I'll hack your leg off!'

Qi Deming laughed, taking my hand and placing it on his chest so that I could feel his pounding heart. 'This heart beats only for you. Anything that came before was just preparation.'

My anger melted away.

Qi Deming's father's printing factory was fairly remote, near to Daowai's large construction material market. It consisted of a tall, narrow cement brick building, around 2000 square meters, with a tin roof. On the west was a warehouse, and on the east was a binding and wallpaper workshop, with the cutting and printing workshop located in the wide space in between. On the left-hand side of the factory stood a perfectly square bungalow, its outer wall painted dark green with a grey tile roof, looking like army barracks. This was the employee dormitory and canteen, Qi Deming told me. We still had ten minutes until we were due to meet his father, so Qi Deming took me to have a look around.

The printing workshop was cleaner and neater than I'd imagined, and the printers were mostly well-known brands like Roland and Heidelberg and not too noisy. The workers wore grey overalls, a style I liked. Some of the workers recognised Qi Deming and greeted him, before stealing a glance or two at me. The air was suffused with ink fragrance, which made me feel warm and relaxed. As I walked towards the paper cutter, Qi Deming suddenly tugged at my sleeve, whispering, 'He's here'.

Qi Deming's father was the man standing in front of the computer-controlled cutter. He was dressed in work overalls, around six foot tall, neither fat nor thin, with hair that was slightly white around the temples, a large square face with reddish skin, single-fold eyelids, sparkly, piercing eyes and slightly upturned nostrils. His wide mouth had straight lines emanating from each corner, which looked like they'd been sliced with a sharp knife and brought out his tough manly side. He shook my hand warmly when he saw me and said, 'You're Xiao'e, I take it. I'm Qi Deming's father, Qi Cangxi!' His hand was course, thick and powerful, the hand of a real man.

I greeted him, not sure what to say after shaking hands. But then Qi Deming piped up with, 'What are you cutting paper for?'

Qi Cangxi patted the paper cutter and said, 'It's a new machine, and it's been giving the workers some grief. It came to a complete standstill, just like that! So I came to teach it a lesson, show it the whip and see if I could tame it!' The way he was speaking made it sound as if the machine was actually a wild horse.

We stood in front of the paper-cutting machine and chatted. I asked Qi Deming's father what he printed, and he told me the main items were brochures, gift bags, calendars, posters and envelopes. Some people approached him about printing fake receipts or pirate copies of books, but he didn't accept any illegal jobs. 'Has Deming told you about how I've been to jail?' he asked with a smile. 'People who've done time appreciate the value of sunlight and freedom more than anyone. No amount of money's worth being stuck back in prison!' Once he'd said this, he wittily turned the topic to my newspaper, saying that if we were looking for a printer, he'd take the job, as save for some slightly exaggerated adverts, it had no improper content.

I laughed, liking Qi Deming's father, how solid and approachable he was; completely different to the image I'd had of him as an arrogant, mercenary type. To become part of their family and have a father-in-law like him would make me very lucky indeed. But I didn't know that fate, the little devil, had already taken the noose and was standing just up ahead, waiting for me.

We went to visit the wallpaper workshop, where we saw a very decrepit-looking older worker.

I put him at around seventy. He was short, skinny and shrivelled, with dark yellow skin, dishevelled hair, a hunched back, a long concave face, small glazed eyes, droopy eyelids and chapped lips. If his fingers hadn't been moving so nimbly I would have thought I was looking at a corpse. When Qi Deming's father saw this man, he was friendlier than he'd been with the other workers. 'Mr Mu, how's your rheumatoid arthritis? Has it flared up this spring?'

Mr Mu's hands stopped what they were doing. He looked at his boss and in a gruff voice said, 'The day it doesn't flare up, I'll be dead!'

'Next time I go to Lindian hot springs, I'll take you to have a good soak,' said Qi Deming's father. 'I've heard that hot springs can be very good for rheumatoid arthritis.'

Mr Mu gave a snort and said, 'There's no cure for this bag of bad bones, not even bathing in liquid gold!'

Everyone laughed at this, including me. Perhaps it was the sound of my laughter that attracted his attention, because at that moment, Mr Mu turned his gaze to me. He shivered when he saw me, as if he'd just been blasted with cold air. Mr Mu lowered his head, gave his eyes a rough rub, and then looked at me again, mumbling the name, 'Yan Yan . . . ?'

Hearing this, Qi Deming's father hurried to introduce me. 'This is Deming's friend, Zhao'e.'

Mr Mu's eyes glistened, and in a shaky voice he asked, 'Where are you from?'

'Keshan,' Qi Deming answered for me. 'Have you heard of the Keshan illness? It's a heart disease that's only been seen in that area. There were lots of cases during the fifties and sixties and lots of people died.'

'Of course, Mr Mu knows about it. That's the illness that ravaged his family,' said his father.

'You're from Keshan too?' I asked Mr Mu in surprise.

Mr Mu looked as if a spell had been cast to turn him to wood, as his body stiffened, his eyes looked like they'd been sealed over and he didn't react in the slightest to my question.

When Qi Deming's father saw what was happening, he gently patted the old man on the shoulder, saying, 'Mr Mu was born in Keshan, but it's been over twenty years since he left. And you haven't been back since, isn't that right?'

Mr Mu shuddered and came to again. 'I have no relatives left there,' he said in a deep voice. 'What reason would I have to go back . . . '

We left Mr Mu, and as we were strolling out of the factory, Qi Deming's father explained to me how Mr Mu's only daughter had been called Yan Yan. She'd gotten sick and died when she was still very young. 'I expect that Yan Yan looked a bit like you and that's why he couldn't stop himself from calling out her name when he saw you,' he explained. He asked me please not to take offence.

We walked towards the employee dormitory. The dormitory had between ten and twenty rooms, all with the same layout. Most of the workers lived four to a room, Qi Deming's father explained; only Mr Mu had his own room due to his age. On the west side of the dormitory was the canteen. The glass door was closed, but delicious smells still wafted out. 'If you don't object, my suggestion would be to have a bite to eat here for lunch,' Qi Deming's father said to me. 'That way you can experience the life of a worker and test out our catering!'

Qi Deming obviously hadn't expected his father's invitation to take us out for a meal to mean at the printing factory canteen. He tugged at his father's sleeve and quietly said, 'It'll be too full and noisy for us to talk properly. Let's go out to eat instead, my treat.'

I, on the other hand, felt that by inviting me to eat with him in front of the workers and introducing me to everyone, Qi Deming's father was showing that he accepted me. 'Let's just eat here,' I said to Qi Deming. 'I enjoy canteen-style food.'

It was the most lively meal I can ever remember having eaten. It certainly wasn't the first time Qi Deming's father had eaten there, as when the workers saw him they said, 'Ah look, the boss eating here again!' The canteen was warm and cosy. It had white walls and ceiling, long chestnut brown tables and benches, light green marble flooring, and two sailing boat-shaped ceiling lamps. Walking through, it gave you the feeling of walking through green grass. We sat down at a long table at the north end of the room, which was the quieter side. Qi Deming and I sat next to each other, opposite his father and Mr Mu. The dishes were all fairly basic. We ordered three main dishes: aubergine with peppers and potatoes, braised yellow croaker, garlic stir-fried primrose gem, accompanied by seaweed soup, rice and steamed Mandarin rolls. The canteen chef was a master and knew just how to bring out the flavour of these hearty, honest dishes. The canteen was filled with the hubbub of workers eating, chatting, and telling the occasional joke, which was met with an eruption of enthusiastic laughter. This pleasant, relaxed atmosphere put me completely at ease and I suddenly felt very hungry. I noticed that most of the workers were men and, was just wondering whether Qi Deming's father discriminated against women, when I remembered what Qi Deming had told me. Most of the workers his father hired had been released from prison after serving their sentences. And in prisons you found significantly more men than women.

My heart gave a lurch as I wondered whether that meant Mr Mu sitting opposite me, who came from Keshan, my hometown, might have been a criminal himself?

Mr Mu was silent while he ate and during the meal, he asked me one question, 'Where in Keshan are you from?' When I told him the county, his hand trembled, and he asked if my village was in the county or outside it. 'Ah,' he said when I told him my village, grimacing and putting down his chopsticks, obviously having bitten his tongue.

Based on his strange reaction, I asked Mr Mu if he knew my village. He stared blankly for a moment before saying, 'Certainly I know it. My old village is right next to yours, only six miles away.'

I remembered visiting his village on my quest to find my mother's rapist and I experienced a twisting sense of foreboding.

Having eaten lunch, the workers left one by one, including Mr Mu. Qi Deming's father went into the kitchen and returned with a pot of jasmine tea and the three of us chatted as we drank it. I took this opportunity to ask more about Mr Mu and was told that he was a man who'd had a very difficult life. His parents and older brother had all died of the Keshan illness and he'd been left orphaned at a young age. A shepherd from his village had adopted him and they had got by relying on each other, until his adoptive father died. At that point, Mr Mu left Keshan for Jixi to find work at the coal mine. After becoming a miner he got married and had a daughter, Yan Yan. But fate could be so cruel and, aged ten, Yan Yan developed leukaemia. Mr Mu bankrupted himself to pay for his daughter's medical treatment and to make matters even worse, the coal mine owner kept withholding his wages. Mr Mu went to the coal mine owner many times to ask for his pay, but with no success. One night, in a state of drunken fury, he took up a chopping knife and headed to the house of this man's mistress, where he took the coal mine owner hostage. He tied him up with rope and, telling him that his hands were stained red with the blood of the miners, he chopped off the thumb and index finger of his right hand – the fingers the coal mine owner used to lick to make it easier to count his money. The coalmine owner had plenty money and he didn't want a penny of compensation from Mr Mu (not that Mr Mu had any to give); he just wanted him to rot in jail. Mr Mu was given a seven-year sentence and during the second year of it, Yan Yan died. His wife accused him of being reckless and irresponsible and proceeded to divorce him on these grounds. Mr Mu was released from jail a wretched and lonely man, for whom the printing factory became home.

I asked Qi Deming's father if Mr Mu was seventy years old.

'Gosh no,' he responded. 'Life has been so cruel that it's left him looking much older than his years. He's actually in his late fifties.'

As we were leaving the printing factory, Qi Deming's father handed his son a shiny key saying, 'You've got your driving licence, don't you? There's a new Citroen parked in the yard behind here. You can drive it away now. It'll make it easier to take Xiao'e out on trips. Remember, I'm lending it to you, not giving it.'

Qi Deming took the key with a grin, but surprised me by merely weighing it in his hand before handing it back to his father, saying he went away on business too much, and it would a shame to see the car turn into a back palace concubine, to be rarely used. Also, he often enjoyed a drink, which you couldn't do if you drove, and he wasn't willing to give up his favourite hobby just so he could drive a car.

'So why did you bother to take your driving test?' Qi Deming's father asked.

'I don't like driving or swimming, but I've learnt how to do them both,' Qi Deming said. 'I'll tell you why. It's simple. If there's a sudden catastrophe, I possess these essential survival skills.'

Qi Deming's father gave his son a bemused look, blissfully unaware that every time the boy went away he carried a shroud in his suitcase.

I I

Spring did not arrive properly in Harbin until the lilac flowers blossomed.

Spring jasmine and peach blossom opened before the lilac, competing to be the first flowers to herald the spring. But Harbin was still cold then, the grass not fully green yet, and most people were still wearing winter clothing. So, these couldn't be the flowers that represented Harbin's spring; they were running on a different calendar.

As soon as the lilac flowers bloomed, that was when the season was changing. The grass was completely green by then and people had packed away their cotton-padded jackets and trousers. The beautiful fragrance of those lilac flowers acted like invisible silver needles, gently prising open pores clogged by the harsh winter and injecting the delightfully warm spring light into your skin, making your body feel extended and relaxed.

When the lilac started to bloom, it went crazy; each tree became like a starry sky, with an impossible number of flowers. At the peak of their flowering, there were so many spikes on the leafstalks that the branches would bend.

The lilacs flowering in this city were mainly purple and white. The purple lilac bushes flowering in the park looked like round purple clouds, while the white lilacs blooming in the streets looked like layers and layers of Mongolian ceremonial scarves. It was a glorious spring, but it might as well have been overcast and gloomy as far as I was concerned. With Qi Deming's help, I started to uncover more information about Mr Mu. What year had he left Keshan? How many times had he been to jail? Qi Deming asked why I was so interested in the man and I explained that he seemed very lonely and helpless. That pitiful way he'd mistaken me for his daughter had got to me and I'd decided to ask him to be my surrogate father. 'I had no idea that Madame Zhao Xiao'e had such a caring side!' mocked Qi Deming.

Through Qi Deming I discovered it was three years after I was born that Mr Mu left his hometown for Jixi. Time-wise, he was a suspect for the crime. More importantly, when he'd left Keshan, he was an adult and unmarried, which made him even more of a suspect.

Just as I had been about to approach Mr Mu, he went missing.

For a whole week, no one had a clue where he was. Qi Deming's father asked everyone who might have seen him, phoned all the places he might have gone, but turned up nothing. Just as he'd been about to report it to the police, Mr Mu came back. When Qi Deming's father asked him where he'd been, he explained that his rheumatoid arthritis had flared up and unable to sleep, he'd gone to Lindian to bathe in the hot springs. But this was one of the places Qi

Deming's father had guessed he might go and he'd called up all of the hot springs resorts, big and small, none of which had a Mr Mu in their books.

Qi Deming heard from his father that Mr Mu had reappeared as elated as someone who'd happened upon some treasure. The man's appetite had improved and he'd become more talkative. He bought some dumbbells, to help straighten his hunched back, he explained. And while working in the workshop, he actually started to whistle. His workmates all thought Mr Mu must have got lucky during his week away and that was why he was in such high spirits.

Qi Deming helped me to arrange a meeting with Mr Mu. The day before we were due to meet, I'd been at work proofreading a newsletter at midday, when I received a call from reception, telling me someone was there to see me. I put down the document and hurried downstairs.

It turned out to be my aunt.

She was wearing a cheap gaudy travel-bag on her back and she had permed her hair. She was wearing green trousers together with a red coat. She had a thick layer of foundation smeared onto her face and so much lipstick her lips looked like erupting volcanoes, while her eyebrows were so heavily outlined they looked like deep crevices. Her ears, neck, wrists and fingers were covered in adornments and she'd put on so much weight, she appeared to be overflowing. 'Dear little Xiao'e,' she said as soon as she saw me. 'It's been so many years and your auntie has been missing you desperately . . . '

I kept to myself in the office and having a spectacle of an aunt suddenly burst in like this made me feel very on-edge. I greeted her and led her straight out of the reception room, deciding to sit down with her at a nearby restaurant and find out why she was here.

On our way to the restaurant, she told me she'd taken a taxi from the train station, but the driver had taken her on a half-hour detour before finally dropping her off at my office – a journey costing her twenty-five *yuan*! She'd asked the old man at the reception at my work, and he'd said that the train station was only a fifteen-minute walk from our office, which should have been the base price in a taxi. She cursed Harbin taxi drivers for their hard hearts.

There were two mauve lilac plants in the restaurant doorway, and as my aunt went through she plucked a couple of flowers and brought them up her nose to sniff. 'The name lilac comes from the word meaning pipe, apparently. You can see why, can't you?' she said.

I couldn't muster up the enthusiasm to talk about flowers with her, so I just gave a perfunctory, 'Yes.'

Aware of how loud my aunt's voice was, I deliberately chose a table in the restaurant's back corner, near the stove and the hatch window, where it was noisy and she could roar as loudly as she liked without upsetting any of the other diners.

As soon as my aunt sat down, she reached out a hand and showed me her shiny ring and bracelet. 'Xiao'e,' she said, lowering her voice. 'I was worried the city folk would look down on me if I wasn't dressed nicely, so I went out especially to buy this gold-plated ring and bracelet. They look just like the real deal, don't they?' She swayed her head to show off her earrings. 'My earrings are the only thing that's real gold. The necklace and brooch are both fake!' She gave a self-satisfied laugh.

'What brooch?' I asked her.

She lowered her head to look at her chest, 'Oh gosh . . .' she cried. 'I was definitely wearing it when I got off the train. It must have dropped in the taxi! Even though it was a fake, it still cost me fifteen *yuan*. Gosh, that taxi really did do me over completely!'

Her look of utter distress made me want to laugh out loud.

I knew my aunt didn't tolerate spicy food well, so I deliberately ordered a fish head with chopped peppers, *mapo* tofu and a spicy-sour soup, with rice. While we were waiting for the food, she complimented me on how beautiful I was looking, before asking me where I lived, how much I earned and whether I got much of a bonus. When she heard I was just renting, she pursed her lips. Her mouth was slightly wonky at the best of times, but when her lips were drawn in like that, she looked truly monstrous and scary. She asked me how many rooms there were at the place I rented and whether there was enough space for her to stay. I told her there wasn't, I only rented one room. Then she asked if I had a double bed she could sleep in with me. The thought made me want to gag and I hurriedly explained that mine was a single bed. Worried she'd suggest sleeping in a makeshift bed on my floor, I launched into how my room was so small you couldn't even turn around in it and I didn't even have the space to fit a chair. My aunt gave a snort and pulled a long face. 'I'll have to find a hotel in that case. I'm not at all familiar with Harbin, so you'll have to help me find one.'

The dishes were all brought out in quick succession, but when my aunt saw that they all contained bright red peppers, her eyes actually lit up, and she explained that she used to hate chillies, but now she couldn't get enough of them. She looked delighted, while my head drooped in dismay. Although she was smacking her lips as she gobbled away, the only words I heard coming from her mouth were complaints: 'They've put too much corn flour in the soup, it's so slimy it's like trying to eat snot!', and 'They haven't dug the gills out of the fish head properly – it absolutely reeks!' and 'This tofu is nothing compared to our Keshan brine-marinated tofu. It's like eating plaster. I saw a group of children playing with slingshots earlier using stones, but this tofu would have worked just as well. This rice is so old it's lost all texture. This restaurant must have bought it on the cheap!'

Once she'd insulted every dish, she asked me if I had a boyfriend. No, I didn't, I told her, shaking my head. She shook her head too, and told me she didn't believe me. When a girl's eyes sparkled like mine, it was always because she'd found herself a boyfriend.

My aunt ate until she couldn't stop burping, before finally putting down her chopsticks and cutting to the chase. The reason she'd come to see me was because an old man had shown up a few days before, asking about illegitimate children from the village. The long-standing villagers knew all about my past, and someone had told this old man about a girl who'd been raped while visiting a grave on Ghost Festival one year and had given birth to a daughter as a result. The man asked where that girl was now. Harbin, they all told him, but she doesn't visit very often. My aunt said that by the time this news had reached her, the old man had left.

'Do you think it might be your biological father trying to track you down?' my aunt asked. 'I was scared that with this information he might come to Harbin to find you. I was worried people might find out and start gossiping about you, so I came here straight away to let you know.'

'Why do you think he's my biological father?' I asked, breaking into a cold sweat.

'Who else would be asking after you?' my aunt said. 'And, when he heard that your mother had died a long time ago, he looked very sad. He bought a big pile of fruit and gave someone a hundred *yuan* to take him to the Western Hills cemetery, where he placed it on your mother's grave.'

I thought back to Mr Mu's disappearance and my heart gave a lurch.

My aunt was monitoring my expression closely the whole time she was telling me this. I was familiar enough with her to know that she wasn't the type to act out of kindness; she had to have an ulterior motive for coming to warn me. I gave a casual smile and told her I wasn't bothered who came to find me. I'd only ever had a mother, never a father. My aunt looked taken aback. She sucked in her lips noisily and finally started to explain that it now looked inevitable that the house I'd grown up in would be pulled down. It seemed a shame not to make use of that big yard in front of the house, and she'd been thinking that with Keshan potatoes being as good as they were, why didn't she set up a factory producing potato-flour noodles. Unfortunately she didn't have start-up funds and was hoping to borrow 30000 from me. Without waiting for a reply, she went on, grumbling about how bad her luck had been over these last few years. First, she'd planned to raise chickens, and had bought a hundred birds, but some freak fowl plague had wiped the whole lot out. After that, her husband had developed diabetes and had to take daily insulin injections that were so expensive it felt like injecting money straight into his veins, making their family poorer by the day. And her son in Qiqihar wasn't exactly doing them proud. After graduating from technical college, rather than exert himself, he'd gotten involved in a pyramid scheme which had backfired. The stress had given him a nervous breakdown and she'd been forced to bring him back to the village and pay his uselessness way. She rubbed her eyes, and upping the emotion, she said, 'With no daughter, I have no one to look after me. I really regret never having a daughter, and I was thinking, Xiao'e, if you don't object, why don't you become my surrogate daughter?'

There was no way I could forget all the humiliation I'd suffered at her hands as a child. My voice came out loud and the tone vengeful. 'Oh, but I do object. There is no way I would take you as my surrogate mother!' My aunt choked when she heard this and stared at me in disbelief. 'And I have no money to lend you in any case,' I continued. 'If you want money, I suggest using your own property as collateral and asking the credit union for a loan.'

'How can you be so disloyal!' my aunt exclaimed. 'In the past, we were family . . .' 'I have no past,' I said. 'I have no past, remember that —'

'If people here knew you were illegitimate, I'm sure they wouldn't look upon you too fondly?' she threatened.

'No one's ashamed of being illegitimate these days,' I sneered in response. 'It's like coming from noble descent, it's very hip!'

I paid the bill, and put 500 *yuan* down in front of her. I told her there was a basic hotel near the restaurant, which cost ninety *yuan* a night if she wanted to stay, but if she preferred not to, she could go back to the train station and get a train home.

'Can't you spend just the afternoon with me?' she asked pitifully.

I was busy with work, I told her, walking stridently out of the restaurant. She followed me out, saying she'd brought me two packets of noodles.

'I can't cook at my lodgings. Give it to someone else,' I said, without even turning my head.

A spring breeze was rippling through the air outside, wafting a floral aroma towards my nose, when all of a sudden an image of Mr Mu's wizened face popped into my mind, and I felt a burst of nausea. If he was my biological father, that made him a criminal who'd raped my mother and there was no way I could forgive him.

I was trudging in through the main entrance of my office, when the old man from reception called out to me. He'd just swept the floor and picked up a brooch, he said. It had only been me and that woman who'd visited him in the reception room that morning, so he assumed that one of us had dropped it. It was an imitation silver brooch shaped like a hyacinth and was the only attractive item out of all my aunt's tacky jewellery.

I took the brooch, explaining to the old man that it belonged to my aunt.

'That aunt of yours is a very interesting lady,' the old man said. 'She was so worried I wouldn't call you that she gave me a packet of dried noodles, but as soon as I'd phoned up and told her you'd be straight down, she packed it away again.'

The old man laughed, but I found myself unable to join in. There was simply too much pain in my chest.

Clutching that brooch, I walked out of the reception room and into the little garden. I chose a bush bursting with purple flowering lilac flowers and placed the brooch underneath. When the purple lilac flowers subsided, like stars in the dawn sky, this hyacinth brooch would allow them to live on.

12

I quickly got close to Mr Mu and started calling him my surrogate father.

Spring that year was a season of darkness for me. Whenever I was with him, I'd be wearing a smile, but I was crying inside the whole time. I carefully examined Mr Mu's facial features to discover that the two of us were actually very much alike; the bean-shaped eyes for example, and the way our mouths turned down ever so slightly while speaking. But most of all it was our ears, which were exactly the same shape, flags of our shared blood, flying ominously between us. I asked to see a photograph of Yan Yan and discovered that we did indeed look like sisters. It was no wonder that Mr Mu had shuddered the first time he saw me, as if seeing a ghost. Even as the fires of vengeance blazed in my heart, I decided to use scientific measures to establish once and for all if we were genetic relations – I didn't want to falsely accuse.

Blood wasn't the only means of testing DNA. Saliva, fingernails and hair could also be used as samples, but it was blood that I wanted. To collect a sample of Mr Mu's blood, I purchased a pack of hairdressing tools, practising on the grass of the gently sloping bank of the Songhua River until I'd mastered the use of the hair clippers. Everyone by the river who witnessed me shearing the grass that day looked at me like I was mad. One overcast Sunday at dusk, when Qi Deming was away on business, I carried my hairdressing tools over to Mr Mu's dormitory. He was delighted when I told him I was going to cut his hair, but asked me please not to take off too much. People who'd done jail time didn't like to have their hair shaved too close, he explained, just as they didn't like wearing vests. He was very quiet as I was shaving him, saying nothing, just emitting the occasional content sigh, as if he was very much enjoying the moment. The hair I'd cut off was like withered grass and had a frosty smell. Just as I was about to finish the shave, I purposefully poked the clippers into the back of his neck, so that its sharp tips stabbed his flesh. The blood started to flow out as anticipated; the blood gathered like a cursed flower, filling me with fear. Mr Mu gave a whimper, but told me not to worry. Even the hands of top hairdressers slipped sometimes, he reassured. I took out a cotton-ball I'd had at the ready and cleaned up his wound, pocketing my blood sample just as planned.

Without proof of identity from a person's workplace, DNA tests would be refused. I went over to Huang Weina's to beg for her help. There was a large vase of beautiful-scented vivid yellow roses on the table by the sofa. She'd just showered and her wet hair was around her shoulders. She was wearing a light green nightdress, and she looked fresh and happy, like she was overflowing with crystal clear water. She told me her birthday had just been and gone, and a new friend had given her the roses. As I was saying what good taste this friend had, she gave a satisfied, 'Yes, he does. He's this big, beefy-looking guy, but his personality couldn't be more different. He's nothing like Doctor Lin – who only ever gave me pink or red roses for my birthday!'

Since Spring Festival, Huang Weina had changed her tactics dealing with Dr Lin, she told me. When the three of them had been skiing at Yabuli, she'd made a point of chatting with other men, skiing with them, drinking rice wine with them, eating pork hotpot and appearing to be having a wonderful time. Dr Lin had pretended not to care, while actually he was being eaten up by jealousy. Now she was no longer the one phoning Dr Lin, she'd stopped her surveillance and didn't follow him and that girl back to where they were staying. Every weekend when he came over to see Lin Lin, she'd make sure to have a different male visitor at the house drinking tea and chatting with her. Dr Lin was enraged by what he saw, but there was nothing he could say.

'Dr Lin is so dumb. He came over once, and as soon the guy I had over left, he started to taunt me by saying, "Huang Weina when did you develop such an appetite? Aren't you worried that with so many different partners you're going to end up with AIDS?"' Huang Weina cackled. 'Even though he's a doctor, he can't see that men are creatures who prioritise physical relationships over emotional ones. The reason I've been changing partners so regularly is that they've all figured out pretty quickly that I wasn't going to sleep with them, and not willing to waste their time, they've gone off to knock at the next door. And anyway, my son was at home, how would that have even been possible!'

Hearing this, I realised that Huang Weina was not feeling as composed as she had first appeared. 'Why are you continuing to torture yourself?' I asked. 'Why not just give up Dr Lin, let him go?'

'Only once I've destroyed him,' she said. 'I'm not going to hand that little hussy a husband full of life and vitality! That bastard says such hurtful things. He hates how healthy I am, God he's tedious. After becoming a doctor he developed a thing for poor little defenceless girls. Tell me, doesn't that sound twisted? When we were dating he liked how clear-headed and healthy I was. I'm going to torture him so much that he's the invalid, then we'll see!' After Huang Weina had finished her rant, she turned her gaze to the yellow roses, and her eyes immediately softened. 'At least there's someone else who likes my health and clear-mindedness,' she said with a sigh. 'Not all men are sewer rats unable to see the sun.'

When I presented Huang Weina with the two blood samples and asked for her help, she stared at me for some time before saying, 'What's going on? If you don't tell me the truth, there's no way I'm going to help you with paternity testing or whatever this is about.'

'Good friends help each other without asking questions,' I said.

'I just need to know if I'm helping you do something good or bad,' Huang Weina replied.

'Something good, of course,' I told her.

'Hmmm . . . ' Huang Weina thought it over for a while before saying, 'okay then. I'll assist you with this underhand activity of yours, but only this once . . . '

'Here's money for the test.' I pulled out 3000 *yuan* from my bag and handed it to her.

'I will need to take the money,' Huang Weina said importantly. 'Business should never be conducted free of charge.

Let's do it this way: if the actual fee is less than 3000, I'll give you the change, and if it's more, you can top it up.'

'Alright . . . ' I said, and added, 'no wonder men like you. You do everything in such a straightforward way – no beating around the bush!'

One June at dusk, after eating in a famous old restaurant in Central Avenue, Qi Deming and I were headed to the banks of the Songhua River for a stroll. As soon as summer arrived, Central Avenue was no longer the place to be, and instead, it was Stalin Park on the bank of the Songhua River people flocked to. You'd be lucky to find a spot on one of the benches beneath the canopy of trees along the path, and even luckier to find space on the stone steps on the riverbank, which were usually colonised by intertwined couples. People selling kites and candyfloss, cold drinks and ice-lollies, parasols and straw hats all saw their business pick up, along with the flow of the river. Qi Deming and I walked along to Jiuzhan Pier and watched as the sunset dyed the river gold. 'We should hire a boat on the river so we can fish for gold bars,' I joked.

Good plan, Qi Deming told me. It would save him having to travel around all over the place selling drugs. While he was asking the boatman how much to hire a boat, I received a phone call from Huang Weina who told me the DNA test results. The two samples of blood I'd given her had tested identical in a number of positions, she explained, which verified genetic kinship between the two people concerned. As soon as I hung up the phone, my teeth started chattering and my whole body trembled. Qi Deming had hired the boat by then. He turned and yelled for me to get in. I walked over to him, tears streaming down my face, as Qi Deming asked again and again what the matter was. I told him the idea of going into the river and fishing out gold bars, going from being poor to being rich had made me so emotional I'd started crying.

'You're lying' Qi Deming said, pursing his lips. 'But you lie with such artistic flare!'

Ji Lianna had once told me that Jewish people saw the sunset as the start of a new day. But that evening, it felt as if the sun for me was setting forever; there'd be no more sunrises to speak of.

I vowed to myself to avenge my mother.

As Qi Deming rowed the boat, I sat in the front, and on this fine evening, surrounded by beautiful nature, I considered all the different ways I might kill Mr Mu. I could feed him dumplings I'd laced with rat poison. I could put sleeping pills in his drink, drug him and then slit his wrists, watch all that dirty blood flow out and then stage it as suicide. I could remove a damaged manhole cover in an unlit section of the road, lead him up to it in the middle of the night and engineer it so he would fell down the hole; a filthy soul would find a fitting end in a filthy sewer. All these methods would be certain to give me away though, and I didn't want to be tried as a murderer and executed. I didn't want to lose Qi Deming. The water lapped against the boat, making a sound like the book pages being turned. It was as if the Songhua River was a great talent, writing magnificent prose with its quill. I suddenly thought; *why not take him off in a little boat to do it?* Mr Mu had told me he was scared of heights and water, but as long as I managed to convince him to get into the boat, I could row him out into deep water at dusk when there was no one about. There, I could catch him off guard and push him in, send him to meet his maker. That way, I could just claim that my surrogate father hadn't been paying attention, lost his balance and fallen from the boat, and because I couldn't swim either, I wasn't able to jump in and save him. This seemed to be the most fail-safe plan.

It was completely dark by the time we were back on the bank. Qi Deming invited me back to stay at his, saying people needed to be intertwined on a night like this. But I turned him down, not in the mood. Qi Deming was so angry that he phoned a bathhouse in front of me and booked himself a masseuse. 'Yes, I'll be there in half an hour. I want a girl who has good hands. Eighteen or nineteen with long hair. Oh, and I don't like girls who smoke, or with sharp nails!'

'Book me a gigolo while you're at it,' I said.

'What specifications do you have?' Qi Deming said, a hissing sound coming from his mouth, like a snake about to attack.

'It would be best if he could . . . ' I paused before spitting out the coarse words, ' . . . fuck me to death.'

'This place only has female prostitutes, no gigolos!' Qi Deming yelled, slapping me around the face. His whole body was shaking as he hugged me. 'Xiao'e, please don't sully yourself just to get your own back on me! How about we get the ferry across the river to Sun Island, hire a tent and spend the night camping there.'

Like a wooden puppet, I allowed myself to be led off, onto the ferry that took us across the river, to the immense darkness of Sun Island. We hired a red and blue tent that looked more like a hot air balloon. That night was like a doomsday carnival, the two of us thrashing around like two fish out of water, covered with sweat, until our bodies were weary.

'What's wrong with girls who have sharp nails?' I asked quietly as I was about to fall asleep.

'Some girls claw wildly at your body as they're in the throes of passion. Sharp nails are like augers, piercing the skin and hurting the flesh.'

Qi Deming's words pierced my heart and hurt its flesh.

Before implementing my murder plan, I went out rowing on the Songhua River several times, practising how to keep the boat steady while paddling. I wanted to avoid capsizing the boat as I was pushing him in the water. In order to keep my cover, I remembered to phone Mr Mu every so often during this time and find out how he was doing.

On one weekend's evening, my chance came.

Mr Mu phoned me out of the blue to say that I wasn't really benefitting from our surrogate daughter-father arrangement. He wanted to set this right by taking me out and buying me a gold necklace. He asked where a good place to do this might be. Central Mall, I said straight away, because it was close to the Songhua River.

The sun was setting by the time we met up. Mr Mu was wearing dark grey trousers and a white T-shirt. He'd shaved and looked very smooth-skinned. He was no longer stooping and his eyes had a gentle glow. I'd seen in the papers that Zhou Sheng Sheng was promoting a new style of the necklace I really liked, I told him. But I'd gone in there while I was waiting, only to be told that Harbin hadn't received the stock yet. I suggested we wait and come back another time to buy it.

'You're right. If we're going to get you one, it should be the one you want. Let's wait!' Mr Mu said cheerfully. 'But since we're at the mall, why don't we go in and take a look around?' he suggested.

He thought I dressed too plainly, he told me, and suggested he buy me a patterned skirt.

'Another day,' I told him, 'I've got a bit of a headache. Why don't we go down to the Songhua River and hire a boat to row around in, enjoy the cool breeze.'

He asked if I'd rowed before. I nodded.

'That sounds great,' he said joyfully.

As we were walking along the river, I automatically found myself stopping each time we passed a lively scene, allowing him one last look. Harbin's Summer Music Festival happened to be on this weekend and Central Avenue had turned into a venue for all these shows. Chamber music was being performed in Modern's beer garden and a saxophonist was playing in front of the Jingu Hotel and had drawn a huge crowd of tourists. Each time Mr Mu moved forward he'd fiddle with his ear, as if it was a blank audio disk he was adjusting in order to record the beautiful music.

By the time we reached Flood Control Monument Pier, hired the boat and got out onto the water, the sun had already set. The water was filled with boats, but it was still a lot quieter than the land. The boat was small, and sat facing each other, him at the front and me at the back, there was only a metre or so between us.

Soon after sitting down in the boat, Mr Mu started getting anxious, but when he realised that I knew how to steer us around without bumping into other boats, he began to relax and sighed contentedly about how much nicer it was on the river than on the shore, no dust, and all this lovely cool breeze. Could I sing, he asked loudly. I shook my head and staring intently into his eyes I said, 'But my mother could.'

He lowered his head. 'Did she sing well?' he asked quietly.

I gave a nod. 'Very beautifully. She only ever sang folk songs.'

'Oh, folk songs, how lovely,' Mr Mu said, his lips trembling.

I rowed our boat to the enormous north bridge, which would obscure my violent crime from everyone. That was where I'd do it, I decided.

The sky gradually darkened and all the pleasure boats started to head back to shore, leaving only the ferries shuttling back and forth. The water surface was dark and wide. There was a hearty river wind, immensely cooling. The noise of the oars pushing through the water didn't sound real at first, but as we moved further from the hustle and bustle and towards solitude, the sound of the roars seemed to swell and expand. I rowed until my whole body was wet with sweat and as we neared the bridge, Mr Mu suddenly asked, 'Do you still have your headache?'

It was a lot better I told him.

'There's a powerful river wind, we should start heading back soon,' he said.

But I couldn't turn back. I still had to deliver him into the water's depths.

Our boat was only a hundred metres or so from the bridge pier, and there were no other boats in sight. A train passed over the bridge, roaring loudly, and it seemed a very opportune moment to do the deed. I quietly set aside the oars and stood up, preparing to lunge towards him. But, who knows whether from sitting down all that time or from fear, my legs started to spasm and I found myself unable to move an inch. In no time the train had passed over the bridge and the boat was starting to rock, but still, I couldn't move. 'Xiao'e, what's wrong with you?' Mr Mu asked, panicking.

'What's wrong with me! How can you not know!' I started sobbing, and out of my mouth slipped the words, 'you've been hiding a crime!'

It was dingy beneath the bridge, but there was a patch of water three meters from the bridge pier reflecting the lights from the bridge, and it looked impossibly exquisite, as if countless numbers of spring flowers had been dropped into the water.

Mr Mu gripped the sides of the boat and turned his head to the watery light reflections. 'I should have known that you knew the whole thing,' he whimpered.

'You raped my mother!' I yelled through my tears. 'Rapists are all assholes who deserve to die.'

The water was still flowing calmly under the bridge, while our boat was churning around. Mr Mu told me to sit down and take hold of the oars, listen to his side of the story. If I still wanted to take his life after that, he wouldn't stop me. In all honesty, I no longer had the strength to carry on standing and Mr Mu's words gave me an excuse to sit down. As he was recounting his story, Mr Mu stroked his face from time to time. He explained that poverty and illness were the two devils that had pushed him into committing his crime.

He'd actually been a very happy child, but that nightmare Keshan illness had stolen his father, mother and older brother from him, and left him an orphan. He was adopted by a shepherd who was kind, but poor, old and ugly; scorned by all women. During Mr Mu's teenage years, his adoptive father had a stroke, and Mr Mu joined the production team feeding livestock and earning work points to support them both. According to Mr Mu, his adoptive father was paralysed, but still conscious and lucid. Seeing his adoptive son maturing, he instructed him to no longer feed the livestock. It was only later that Mr Mu learned from a neighbour the reason his adoptive father had said this. It was because he was afraid his son wouldn't find a wife either apparently, and might become lured into bestiality. 'Men are men. They are not meant to have sex with beasts,' Mr Mu explained in a shaky voice.

His village was so poor that it made our village seem prosperous, he told me, and each year at Grave Sweeping and Ghost Festivals, he'd walk along the Wuyuer River to arrive in our village cemetery at dusk and once there, he would steal the grave offerings. One year he swept up half a sack of steamed buns to take home. If he was really lucky, he might pick up some smoked meat, eggs, fish steaks, apples, cigarettes, toffee apples and other such offerings. He'd never come across anyone while doing this, because everyone had paid their visits by the time he got there. But that year's Ghost Festival he came across a woman at Eastern Hills cemetery, and fell in love with her at a glance. She had full red lips and watery eyes, and was wearing a close-fitting blue patterned shirt. She was absolutely adorable and he couldn't stop himself; he rushed over and grabbed her.

'Didn't she struggle?' I asked trembling.

'She did struggle,' Mr Mu said, 'But when I told her my age and that I'd never been near a woman, and explained that if she didn't agree, I'd end up fucking a lamb, becoming no better than a beast myself, she stopped struggling. But even though she submitted to me, she didn't stop shaking and neither did I.'

'You disgust me!' I yelled.'You should be struck by lightning, trampled to death by livestock and torn apart by wolves!'

'Xiao'e. Can you not find it in yourself to forgive me? I will surrender myself, own up to my crime and serve the sentence the court sets me! For you, I am prepared to spend the rest of my life in prison, and willingly.'

'If you give yourself in, I'll be implicated! Do you think I want people knowing that I'm the daughter of a rapist! What planet are you on!'

'I understand . . .' Mr Mu said, his voice calm once more.

Before he cast himself into the river, he handed me his wallet and told me he had a Union bank card inside. He had 50 000 *yuan* in the account and hadn't set up a pin number. When I got married, I could use it to buy something for myself. The last words he said to me were, 'Row back carefully, and get a taxi home from the shore, you shouldn't walk on your own at night.'

Mr Mu leapt into the waves. The moon was out by the time I started rowing away from the bridge. The moon that night looked like a lonely ghost: deathly, deathly pale.

13

Mr Mu's body was discovered in the Daowai section of the river.

I returned to the pier that evening and reported the incident to the police. My surrogate father hadn't been sitting down steadily in the boat, I told them, and had fallen into the water by the bridge. The lifeboat made its way to the bridge and followed the river downstream, searching. They found him floating on the surface of the moonlit river like a black fish.

The police had their suspicions about me and the forensics team carried out an autopsy of his body. The results showed that Mr Mu had suffered no trauma or internal injuries and had died from drowning.

Qi Deming's father bought a plot of land at the Huangshan public cemetery and arranged a burial for him there.

I'd imagined that once he was dead, I'd feel that I'd avenged the grudge I'd nurtured over all those years, and experience a sense of release, but actually this was not the case. Unable to eat or sleep, I spent my days in a trance and made constant mistakes at work. With a red pen, I'd repeatedly tick and underline the parts of the text I wasn't meant to proofread and arbitrarily change things in the draft, while blindly overlooking the actual mistakes. The most terrible thing was when I accidentally deleted a letter of a keyword in the front-page editorial so that 'flag nation' became 'fag nation'. Luckily it was the deputy editor on duty, an extremely meticulous worker, who noticed this glaring error and was able to correct it before the paper went to print. The boss was furious and called me in for a talk, during which he told me that as a professional proof-reader, such mistakes were unforgivable. If such a thing had happened during the Cultural Revolution I would have been considered a political criminal and thrown in prison. Any more mistakes like that and the newspaper would have to let me go.

My job was the only security I had, so after that incident, whenever I proofread, I would stare at each and every character as intensely as a long-departed mother at her children. I looked them over so many times that my eyes would ache, and I had to use eye drops several times a day.

I had no interest in food, and my face became pallid and gaunt. I no longer took any care over what I wore to work, turning up in odd socks, my shirts and skirts creased and my buttons done up in the wrong buttonholes. The worst was at night when I suffered nightmare after nightmare, often causing me to cry out, waking Ji Lianna.

Qi Deming attributed my strange behaviour to the shock of having witnessed Mr Mu's drowning. He eagerly tried to find me another surrogate father, explaining that while I could only ever have one birth father, the world was teaming with surrogate fathers waiting to be introduced to me.

Huang Weina was the only one with an inkling of what was going on with me, but even she didn't know the actual facts. All she was aware of was that it had something to do with the DNA test. If she'd known it was going to have this effect, she never would have agreed to help me, she said. In this troubled world, ignorant people enjoyed happy lives while the knowledgeable lived in agony. She suggested that I go on sick leave for a while. The characters on the page were tormenting me so much by that point that I'd become physically and emotionally drained, and as I proofread I'd begun to doubt every character. On the brink of collapse, I finally took Huang Weina's advice and asked to go on sick leave.

I still had the bankcard Mr Mu had given to me, which I had hidden under my bed frame just after the incident, but never had the courage to use. While on sick leave, I took it out and placed it in my purse. I went to Central Mall and followed Mr Mu's wishes by buying myself a patterned skirt. As I swiped the card for the first time, my heart was racing and my breath short. I glanced all around me, just like a thief. When signing Mr Mu's signature on the transaction sheet, his actual name, Mu Changkuan, the pen in my hand started shaking, but the transaction went through successfully and I walked away with the patterned skirt. After this, my courage doubled and the next time I used it I was composed and poised, as if it had always been mine. I started to go on crazy shopping sprees: I bought a gold necklace, a mobile phone, a jasper bracelet, high-quality leather shoes and a pair of sunglasses. In one week I'd managed to completely transform my appearance, and spent over 10 000 *yuan*. As well as shopping, I took myself to fancy restaurants where I experienced fine dining, as most restaurants accepted swipe cards by then. I adored the taste of crayfish cooked with chillies and Sichuan peppercorn, so spicy it turned my lips a brilliant red, so red that I didn't even need lipstick. Qi Deming noticed that I'd started dressing seductively and was constantly acquiring new and expensive things, and assumed I was up to no good. In his eyes, a girl who wasn't particularly attractive and had a weird temperament like mine wouldn't be able to get a sugar daddy. And if I didn't have a sugar daddy and hadn't won the lottery, there was only one explanation for how I'd managed to suddenly become so extravagant – I must be working as a prostitute.

Qi Deming started giving me the cold shoulder, but I couldn't let him go. I went to Zhongshan Gardens one day without prior arrangement. After taking a shower, I opened his suitcase and draped his shroud over my body before running into show Qi Deming, who was in bed anticipating our passion. He hid his face in the quilt in fear and let out a piercing cry. 'You ghoulish girl . . . ' He stopped talking to me after that.

I'd satisfied my material life, but mentally I was still on a cliff's edge. I took Valium every night, but still didn't manage to sleep properly. I saw flashes in front of my eyes, suffered auditory hallucinations and often felt as if my brain was filled with a big white space. Late one night I dreamt about Mr Mu. He was thin to the point of almost being unrecognisable and dressed entirely in rags, his feet bare. His face was as pale and thin as paper and covered in stubble, and his eyelids drooped. He was holding an empty cup and walking down the road begging for food. When he knocked at my door and saw me, he wept unashamedly and called out, 'Oh, my daughter . . .'

I awoke from the dream covered in sweat, stared up at the dark ceiling, and promptly burst into tears. Ji Lianna was startled awake. She turned on the hall light and pushed open the door to my room. Seeing her in that milky yellow light with her white silk nightgown over her skeleton-thin body and her hair hanging loose was a shocking sight, and I shrieked out in terror. Ji Lianna walked over. 'Don't be scared, Xiao'e. It's me, Ji Lianna,' she said softly.

'Ji Lianna!' I cried out and threw myself into her arms. 'Ji Lianna, please save me!' I begged.

Ji Lianna gently stroked my hair. 'Have you lost your job?' she asked quietly.

'No,' I said, 'but I fear it may happen soon . . .'

'Has that drug salesman broken up with you?' she asked.

'I wore his shroud one day and scared him witless,' I told her. 'But that wasn't the only thing.'

'Is there something wrong with your health, Xiao'e?' Ji Lianna clasped my shoulder and stared at me. 'You haven't been looking at all well recently and you've been spending money at an alarming rate. Are your days . . . numbered?'

'No, that's not it!' In the end, I couldn't keep it in. 'I forced my biological father to commit suicide,' I told Ji Lianna. 'I killed him.'

Ji Lianna stared wide-eyed and then took back her hand. She stood up stiffly, her face pale, and slowly walked away. In no time I could hear the sound of praying coming from her room. I could smell the faint scent of the flowers in the hall, and as her prayers floated through the floral aroma, they became like spring jasmine branches, covered in exquisite flowers.

Ji Lianna finished praying and went to the kitchen to prepare refreshments, which she carried out to the small table by the piano before calling me over. We sat opposite each other, drinking green tea, eating salty cheese and began our long discussion. I told her everything that had been buried deep inside me, keeping nothing back. And after she'd heard all of my life's misfortunes, she shared her deeply hidden secrets with me.

Ji Lianna revealed that she and I were the same in that we'd both killed our fathers. The only difference was that I had killed my real father, while hers had been her step-father.

Ji Lianna's stepfather had married her mother during the era when northeast China was a puppet state ruled by the Japanese. All the Jews who'd been exiled to Harbin nurtured a Zionist dream and some of them rested this hope on the Japanese, who secretly promised to allow them to realise it on Chinese soil.

Ji Lianna's stepfather was a businessman, she told me, but it wasn't just Japanese businessmen he was in contact with, he had connections with people from the Japanese political and military worlds too and often took them out to New World or Modern to entertain them. The summer that Ji Lianna turned eighteen, her stepfather entertained a guest at home for the first time. This man came from Shinkyo and had a high-ranking position in the Kwantung Army Headquarters. He was passing through on his way to Manzhou, where he was going to inspect the border fortifications. This Japanese man was a decade older than Ji

Lianna; he was short and slim, with eagle eyes. He was stern, with a gloomy temperament, and he spoke fluent Chinese. During their dinner, her stepfather called Ji Lianna in to play a piece on the piano. She chose Schumann's *Scenes from Childhood*.

Ji Lianna told me how shocked she had been when following this meeting, the army officer had returned to Harbin from Manzhou especially to pay them a visit at home and ask for her hand in marriage. Her mother didn't want her daughter to marry a Japanese man or to leave Harbin, but her stepfather was elated. He said that were Ji Lianna to marry someone of such high ranking, it would be hugely beneficial to the Zionist cause and he tried his best to convince Ji Lianna's mother. But Ji Lianna was resolute; she would not marry a soldier and especially not a Japanese soldier. Her stepfather appeared to respect her decision, but actually, he was hatching a plan to hand Ji Lianna over.

The night before the Japanese army officer left Harbin, her stepfather told her that the railroad entertainment club had a singing performance. Knowing how much she liked the Jewish folk songs sung by this female singer, he invited Ji Lianna to go with them. Ji Lianna was surprised to see the Japanese officer waiting for them at the club, seated right next to her. No wonder her stepfather had said that there were no more tickets when Ji Lianna's mother had expressed interest in joining them. Once the performance was over, they all left the entertainment club and got in the same taxi. Her stepfather explained that they would drop their guest off at his hotel first and so the taxi drove towards the Grand Hotel. It was getting late and there were few cars on the street, and hardly any streetlights.

They arrived at the entrance to the hotel and the Japanese officer invited them to join him for a drink and her stepfather accepted eagerly. Ji Lianna joined them, assuming that she'd be safe in her stepfather's company. The Japanese officer hosted them in his hotel room and ordered a waiter to bring them refreshments. Ji Lianna's stepfather asked her what she wanted to drink. She looked at what they had, and from the sake, coffee and tea she chose a cream coffee. As she picked up the cup and took a sip, her stepfather reminded her to wash her hands. Ji Lianna went off to do so. She returned and finished her coffee, immediately starting to feel herself go floppy. She became increasingly drowsy and everything started to blur. She shouted that she wanted to go home, but her stepfather ignored her, leaving her there. At that moment she understood what had happened: they'd drugged her coffee. She awoke the next morning to find herself lying naked in a hotel bed next to the Japanese army officer. He readily confessed, saying he was in love with her, in love with her piano playing and hoped to marry her. 'I'd never agree,' Ji Lianna told him, 'not even if you held a gun to my head.' Just as she was struggling out of the bed, her stepfather arrived. He had gone back home the night before and told his wife that Ji Lianna had bumped into her classmate Natasha during the performance and had gone back to stay at her place. Ji Lianna and Natasha were good friends, they both played the piano together and studied art, and in the past she used to stay over at Natasha's, so Ji Lianna's mother didn't find this strange. Her stepfather had imagined that once the Japanese army officer had his way with her, Ji Lianna would be humbled enough to agree to marry him. He hadn't realised that she would rather die. Ji Lianna said that from that point on, she wanted to kill him. She couldn't bear her mother being with such a ruthless man. The Japanese officer returned to Shinyko after that, but he still thought about Ji Lianna constantly and came back to Harbin to see her a couple of times. Ji Lianna realised that his infatuation was not wearing off and she started to act as if she were crazy. The trick worked; when the Japanese officer saw how strangely she was behaving, he turned around and was gone. She was a superb actress, Ji Lianna joked, even managing to fool her mother and stepfather.

Once the Japanese officer had disappeared from her life, Ji Lianna started to hatch her revenge plan. Her stepfather had become addicted to opium, but he never went to opium dens, only ever taking it at home. He had set up a room, which he called the hospitality tearoom, but was actually his opium den. He had two large opium pipes laid across the redwood table like precious objects. One of them had a timber bamboo body, a silver head, a jade mouthpiece and a claw-shaped red-clay smoking pipe. The other was made from African rhino horn, carved with pictures of bats and rock chrysanthemums, the mouthpiece made from elephant tusk ivory and the head coated in gold leaf, with a hexagonal pipe all six sides of which were encrusted with rubies. They were utterly beautiful, utterly magnificent pipes and her stepfather adored them both. He would lie down on his chaise-long and heat the opium resin. Whenever he was puffing away in ecstasy, the rest of the family knew not to disturb him.

It was these two pipes that gave Ji Lianna her idea. She wanted to kill him without his knowledge. She bought some arsenic, and every second week she would use a toothpick to push a little down through the mouthpiece and into the pipe body, setting up his death trap. The arsenic lay in wait inside the pipe, while she waited each day for it to be absorbed into her stepfather's blood. Ji Lianna said that from that point on, her stepfather would be in a bad state for a couple of days each time he smoked opium, but the worse he felt, the more he wanted it. He became fretful, emaciated, coughing a lot and suffering chest pains, until finally, one day after smoking opium, on his way to Songpu foreign firm for work, he suddenly fell down dead. Everyone just assumed that the cause of death was an opium overdose, Ji Lianna's mother included, so the body was put straight in a coffin. After his burial, Ji Lianna stopped pretending to be crazy and returned to her normal self. Despite how valuable those two pipes were Ji Lianna's mother hated them, blaming them for damaging his mind. She put them in the furnace and incinerated them. The thing that pained Ji Lianna the most were the rubies encrusted on the six sides of the pipe gourd. Not long after the death of her stepfather, the Japanese declared unconditional surrender and the northeast was recovered. Ji Lianna read in the newspaper that the Japanese officer who had raped her had died by committing harakiri the day before the great exodus. It was at this time that she experienced the dawning of love. This dawn shone down on the horizon of her soul and never again had it set throughout all those years of her life.

Ji Lianna was born and grew up in Harbin, and both her Russian and Chinese language skills were excellent. When the Soviet Army moved into Harbin, she was hired by the Soviet Consulate to work as a translator and participated in some post-war affairs. This was how Ji Lianna met her Russian diplomat. He was noble and refined, ten years her senior, and loved music and painting just as she did. She knew he had a family in the Soviet Union and would be leaving China soon, but all the same, she couldn't help herself from falling in love. I asked her for this foreign diplomat's name, but Ji Lianna wouldn't say; all she would tell me was that he was like her, another talented actor: he had successfully managed to trap the White-Russian reactionary pro-Japanese leader, who was arrested and taken back to Moscow, where he was thrown into Lubyanka prison.

During their last night together in Harbin, the Soviet Diplomat invited Ji Lianna to eat with him at Modern, where he gave her a snowflake brooch. They danced and drank together. Ji Lianna said that he really knew how to lead on the dance floor. His dance style was bold but gentle, and dancing in the crook of his arm, she felt as if she were a cloud. They said goodbye and never met again.

'Didn't you even send letters?' I asked.

Ji Lianna shook her head. 'During your last night together, when you danced with him, did you wear your hair in a braid?' I asked.

'How did you know?' she asked in surprise.

'When you invited me to eat at Modern on New Year's Day, that's how you were wearing your hair,' I said. 'And the brooch you were wearing must have been the one he gave you.'

Ji Lianna pursed her lips and gave a bashful smile.

'You were only twenty at the time, it couldn't have been easy to recover from a love like that,' I asked.

'Xiao'e, laugh at me if you will, but I was in agony after he went back to the Soviet Union. I cried myself to sleep every night and became so thin that I barely looked like me. I was scared I really had gone crazy. The next March I went down to Hangzhou by myself to see the Xiangxue Hai plum blossom. I stood in the plum orchard, and looked at the plum blossom flowering and falling, and realised that true love was like flowers, it lasts for a time and then is gone. I could see it for what it was. I actually started to blossom then and the aromatic aftertaste of that love has remained with me inside my heart throughout my whole life.'

I understood now why Ji Lianna had not buried her mother and stepfather together. I asked her if she still hated her stepfather. After a long pause she said, 'I killed him and I've had to wash clean my sin.'

'Is it still a crime if it's a demon you kill?' I asked fretfully.

Ji Lianna didn't respond, she just turned around and went back to her room and returned with the rattan box inlaid with the Star of David. She told me that inside it, along with her Hebrew Scripture, she kept the brooch given to her by the Soviet Diplomat and a sachet she'd sewed herself, filled with the plum blossom she'd picked during that visit to Xiangxue Hai all those years ago. She asked me if I could carry out some instructions when she died. I was to wrap her body in white material and cremate her with her brooch and sachet, while her rattan box and Hebrew Scripture should be donated to the New Synagogue. She said that her lawyer would be in charge of executing all her assets, including the house; but she'd prefer if I was responsible for the items in the rattan box.

I told her I would. By then it was already getting light outside.

14

Harbin's summer put a real strain on the city's wardrobes. Those thick and heavy winter clothes were already taking so much space inside them and now the spring clothing was stuffed in there as well, narrowing the space even further, while the mothballs put in there to prevent infestation gave off an unpleasant odour, suffocating these wardrobes further still.

But the plight of these wardrobes didn't matter much, not when all the women were all in such high spirits.

It was rare to meet a woman who didn't like summer, a season that allowed them to start dressing in an array of slinky silk and satin strapless tops. Some married women complained about summer because people tended to sweat more and their family members needed their vests washed daily. It was also during this season that the men loved to enjoy a cold beer. They would spend their evenings sitting out in small groups at bars in the night market, sustaining themselves with fried snacks and mixed cold dishes, continuing to drink well into the night, leaving the women feeling left out at home. That may have been the case, but after the women had finished their housework, and gone to bed early and had a good night's rest, when they woke up the next morning feeling refreshed and had changed into their cool and sleek summer outfits and admired their elegant reflections in the mirrors, their moods soon cleared.

But I didn't dare to wear revealing summer clothing, such as miniskirts, bright coloured V-neck T-shirts, short sleeves, stonewashed denim shorts and strappy sandals. These used to be my favourite items, but that summer they fell into disfavour and found themselves shunned. I started to buy conservative summer wear instead. All my shirts were now long-sleeved and buttoned up all the way to the top, while my skirts so long they dragged along the ground and could have been used to mop to the floor. I exchanged my strappy leather sandals for long-tongued shoes that hid the toes. I kept my body more concealed than a nun, not allowing even an inch of exposure to the sunshine.

After telling Ji Lianna my dark secret, I felt as if I'd found an accomplice. I no longer felt flooded with all that panic, my nightmares came more rarely and I was starting to feel more relaxed. The opposite seemed true for Ji Lianna, who began to seem even glummer than before, and would often look at me blankly. I assumed she regretted telling me her story, perhaps worrying that her secret was no longer safe. I reassured her, saying that even though I worked for a newspaper, I wasn't one of those unscrupulous reporters and would never dream of writing about her experiences or telling her secret to another soul.

When Ji Lianna heard this, she finally revealed what had been on her mind. She wasn't concerned about herself, but about me. Even though I'd forced my father to his death, she couldn't see me showing any repentance and this made her feel terribly afraid. A person who didn't understand repentance, would be unable to see the dawning of the other world, she explained. I thought about what Qi Deming had once told me, that it had been that deep sense of hopelessness in my eyes that had chimed with him and initially sparked his interest. Which, according to Ji Lianna's words, meant he was another person who wouldn't get to see the dawning of the other world.

Ji Lianna told me that during the early 1950s, following Israel's 1948 declaration of independence, a steady stream of Jews started to leave Harbin and return to Israel, but she hadn't felt the impulse. It wasn't just the warm arm Harbin had extended to the Jews during their persecution; it was also because all of her love and all of her hate resided here. The love she'd experienced here had made it her home, while her hate had been the baptism she'd received from *Him*. A person had to eliminate hate before they could be touched by an angel's wings and before they received *His* blessing. She told me that in over half a century her love hadn't changed, while the hate she felt towards her stepfather had diminished day by day. The world we live in felt so dark, and I didn't believe there was another world filled with light, I told Ji Lianna.

Ji Lianna told me that this world was half darkness and half light. *He* provided the darkness and the light for human beings to trek through, to clearly show them that there were two paths, one of eternal light, and one of eternal darkness.

'So it's heaven and hell you're talking about? But if heaven is as bright as you say, I won't be able to tolerate it anyway, because I'm allergic to UV,' I said flippantly. 'I find the idea of hell a lot less scary to be honest. And haven't

I already been to hell? I'm not afraid of going back down again.' Tears were pouring from my eyes as I said this.

Ji Lianna was also crying, but she still managed to speak. 'Xiao'e, I've been thinking it through. What your father did to your mother at the cemetery all those years ago wasn't completely unforgivable. Didn't your mother herself feel sorry for him and end up submitting to him?'

'What are you saying, he didn't rape her and I shouldn't have killed him?' I said. 'What's your justification for poisoning your stepfather with arsenic in that case!'

'It's as I've told you,' Ji Lianna said compassionately. 'I've already washed away my sin.'

'Well, I haven't sinned!' I sneered. 'You can't blame me. I was conceived in a cemetery. I'm a ghost in human form!'

Ji Lianna made a sound of exasperation and stood up as quickly as I'd ever seen her. With a lightning strike of the hand, she slapped me across the face, before leaning against me like dead wood and crying. It was the first time I'd seen her weep. When she released me, she brought her mouth up to my cheek and said, 'I'm sorry, I shouldn't have hit you. I just wanted you to understand mercy. Mercy can bring a person peace and joy. Also, who dresses like this in the summer? Please don't view all men as rapists.'

Feeling Ji Lianna's face up against mine caused a searing pain in my heart. Her cheek felt like a crisp mid-autumn leaf, exceptionally dry. That light brush against me had been like an earthquake, instantly disintegrating her skin. When a woman loses her moisture, it is a sign that death is near. I was terrified of her leaving.

From then on, I noticed Ji Lianna's body becoming steadily weaker. In the past she'd never slept very well, but now she found it hard to stay awake. By the time she'd dragged herself drowsily up from bed, it would be to witness the scorching midday sun. She would brush her hair, have a wash and eat something, and then spend the whole afternoon in her room praying. Her two meals a day became one, taken at dusk, and the furthest she ventured out now was downstairs for a cup of coffee. She no longer played the piano, but still tended those poor plants and flowers in the hall and on the balcony, never forgetting to turn their soil or water them.

At the time that Ji Lianna was most in need of someone to care for her, Huang Weina asked me to stay at her place and look after Lin Lin.

Huang Weina was accompanying a visiting economy and trade delegation from Hong Kong, and had gone off to Great Northern Wilderness to conduct interviews. She didn't feel comfortable leaving Lin Lin with Doctor Lin, she explained, scared the little artist hussy would harm her child and so she asked me if I'd look after him for the week, seeing as I was still on sick leave. I stayed at hers to look after Lin Lin but still went to see Ji Lianna each day, buying a little bread and fruit to take over. She was gradually losing function in her legs and when she walked her body would be tilted forwards, her top half overhanging, while her legs looked like they'd been caught in a snare and her movements very arduous. Ji Lianna accepted the bread and the fruit, but would always ask me how much and repay every penny. And whenever I got distracted and forgot to pay my monthly water, gas and electricity bill, she wouldn't have any qualms about looking at me square on and just demanding it back. She wanted every bill settled with no outstanding payments. The day before Huang Weina was due to return was a Sunday, so Lin Lin was off school and could enjoy a little lie-in. After getting up, we both had a bowl of egg noodles. It was a blistering hot day and I told him that if he came with me to see Granny Ji Lianna, afterwards we could visit the Polar Museum on Sun Island and see the penguins. Lin Lin hadn't seen Ji Lianna since Passover and he seemed very excited. He told me he wanted to give Granny Ji Lianna a nice surprise by dressing up like Moses.

What did Moses look like? I imagined him dressed in black, with a red cloak and a black top hat. All Lin Lin could remember was that Moses had a staff. He didn't want to look for his outfit with me, but instead ran to the storage room to look for a staff. A while later he came back with a red sandalwood walking stick, which he told me used to be his grandfather's. His mother had kept the stick so that when she was old with no one to look after her, it could act as her son. 'A walking stick can't talk so how can it be like a son?' Lin Lin asked. I told him it couldn't. 'A son can kiss his mother and talk to her, can a walking stick do that?' asked Lin Lin. Hearing these words stimulated my maternal desire and I felt an unbearable longing for Qi Deming.

It was noon when we arrived at Ji Lianna's. Lin Lin was wearing a white shirt and black trousers, with a curved-brim cowboy hat on his head and the walking stick in his hand. It was a hot day and at the street corner we decided to buy a watermelon, planning to cut it up once we were inside for Ji Lianna to eat.

Lin Lin had a plan: we would go upstairs and I would quietly unlock the door, letting him in while I stayed outside, so he could give Ji Lianna her surprise.

As soon as the door was open, Lin Lin snuck inside, aided by his walking stick. I heard him chanting, 'Mo-o-o- Ses-es-es Is-is-is Here-ere-ere' giving the words an outer space reverberation. I heard Ji Lianna give a little laugh, followed by a muffled thump and then Lin Lin crying out in alarm.

Ji Lianna had fallen to the ground. She had been using her spray bottle to water the in bloom michelia and as she fell the bottle had sprayed her in the face. There was the hint of a smile on her face and her dry skin was drizzled with water droplets, making her look like she was covered in dew. As if this wasn't already a pretty enough picture, a few yellow petals had floated down and landed onto her, their wilted forms giving a hint of fragrance to usher Ji Lianna into the next world.

Ji Lianna had given me her lawyer's number sometime before, saying that the first thing I should do when she died was to call him and he would take care of things from there. So that's what I did.

Ji Lianna's lawyer was in his fifties, a fellow music enthusiast, who came across as calm and knowledgeable. We followed Ji Lianna's wishes, wrapping her body in white material and cremating her along with her brooch and her sachet of plum blossom. She was buried in the Jewish cemetery beside her mother. After the funeral, the lawyer gave me a detailed description of her will. Not long before she died, Ji Lianna had made a last minute change to her will relating to the attribution of her house, he explained. She'd donated her piano and her music books to the school where she used to teach. She'd donated her bank savings of 210 000 *yuan*, minus the funeral expenses and lawyers fees, to an old age home. Her biggest legacy was her apartment, and I had no idea who she'd been planning to leave it to before and for what purpose, and neither did her lawyer disclose this information. All I was privy to was that in the very last moment of her life, Ji Lianna had changed her will to name me this house's sole inheritor.

The moment her lawyer announced that this would be my house, I felt as if I'd just landed on an immensely high plateau: my heartbeat sped up, my breath became shallow, my cheeks burned, I felt as if my brain was being starved of oxygen and everything went white. When the lawyer took out the real estate license and land certificate Ji Lianna had left and asked when he could take me to carry out the house transfer procedure, I suddenly felt terrified that it was all just a dream. 'Now! Let's just go now . . .' I kept saying.

I finally had my own home in Harbin! I couldn't quite take in how such good fortune had come my way. I called my brother to tell him the news and he came to see me that very same night. He arrived at my place clammy with sweat, and after a very quick hello, he wandered around the house like a police officer with a search warrant, carefully inspecting every nook and cranny. He let out a long sigh when he was done, walked out onto the balcony and lit a cigarette. In a voice racked with sobs he said, 'Xiao'e, as your older brother I would have been willing to break my back to look after you, but now it looks like I won't need to. You must know how expensive houses in Harbin are? I knew you wouldn't be able to afford one yourself and so I wanted to help you out. I've already saved up 70 000 *yuan* for you.'

I grabbed my brother's hand, tears splashing down my cheeks.

Harbin's summers were usually very short, but that summer left a very deep impression on me. During mid-August, the streets were still full of people dressed in short sleeves and strappy sandals. I'd been living alone in the house left to me by Ji Lianna for two weeks by then. I woke up every morning and walked a circuit around each room, like a mule pulling a mill. Even though the real estate license had my name on it by then, I still couldn't believe this place was mine. I didn't move any of Ji Lianna's things; apart from the piano and the books that had gone, everything was kept exactly the same as when she was alive. The photos of her and her family were still on the mantelpiece and each time I walked through the hall, I would feel her gaze. I could still hear the sound of her prayers reverberating in my ears. Whenever I drank tea, I was still in the habit of laying out two teacups and each time I left the house, I would call out, 'Ji Lianna I'm heading out now,' just like before. The only change was that the flowers she had tended so carefully, in the hall, on the balcony and in the bedroom, were becoming more withered by the day. I always remembered to water them, turn their soil and add fertilizer, but still they moved towards deterioration. I believed that these flowers missed their mistress and were following Ji Lianna.

I started to think that Ji Lianna might have been right; that there was a place we were unable to see with the naked eye where another world existed. I started to reflect on what I'd done to my biological father. Had his sins really been unforgivable? Why then after getting the revenge I believed he deserved, did I still feel upset? I went over that night out on the Songhua River again and again in my mind, remembering the way he'd begged me to find it in myself to forgive him. His voice had been so forlorn and beseeching, and I felt a pain in my chest so immense it was as if my heart was being torn apart. I phoned Qi Deming's father, and asked how much he had spent on Mr Mu's grave. Seventy thousand *yuan*, he said. I took out 20 000 from my biological father's bank account – all of what was left after all my squandering. I added to that my own money, saved up through frugal living, and managed to scrape together 70 000. One rainy weekend, I took a taxi to the print factory and handed it over to Qi Deming's father. I said that as Mr Mu's surrogate daughter, I felt I should be the one to pay for his gravesite. He must have seen something in my eyes, because he said, 'If I accept this money and it gives you some peace, on Mr Mu's behalf, I will do so.'

As we were saying goodbye, Qi Deming's father suddenly said, 'Xiao'e, I heard that the old Jewish lady you were living with left you her house. If you don't feel comfortable living there, you could always sell it. I could help you buy somewhere else. Houses in that area are worth a lot – you won't find it hard to sell.'

I was very surprised. It had been a long time since Qi Deming and I had been in touch, so how could he have known? I asked a few questions, until finally Qi Deming's father mentioned Huang Weina. He was a bit hesitant, saying that when he'd first met Huang Weina, he didn't know we worked at the same newspaper office, or that we were friends. Huang Weina had told him she worked for a publicity company. It was only when he'd been watching a news item on television and seen her accompanying the Hong Kong economic and trade delegation and holding interviews in the Great Northern Wilderness that he discovered her true identity. From the way he was talking about her, I could tell that they shared something special.

'Were you the one who gave Huang Weina those yellow roses for her birthday?' I asked.

He nodded.

'Does Qi Deming know about this?' I asked.

'I've told him,' he said.

'What did he say?'

'Not much,' said Qi Deming's father.

After saying goodbye I strolled along the Songhua River from Daowai all the way to Huang Weina's in Daoli. I'd forgotten my umbrella at the print factory and the rain drizzled down onto my head as I walked. It actually felt quite good being sprinkled with rain, as no one could tell I was crying. The Songhua River had become a mass of misty rain and drizzle, and my heart was a mass of misty rain and drizzle, too. After walking for an hour or more, I arrived at Huang Weina's.

Huang Weina looked exhausted and her complexion was terrible. She told me that, since Ji Lianna's death Lin Lin had become terrified of walking sticks, and whenever he saw someone in the street with one, he'd turn around and run. He believed that walking sticks could kill people. He'd become so scared recently that he wouldn't even go outdoors and Huang Wei was worried he might be developing autism.

I felt like I'd really let Huang Weina down. I was the one who'd helped Lin Lin dress up as Moses, and let him carry the walking stick in to see Ji Lianna.

'I know why you've come, Qi Canxi just called . . .' Huang Weina handed me a cotton nightdress and told me I'd better change out of my wet clothes or I'd get a chill. Then she lit a cigarette and said, 'Zhao Xiao'e, you kept your boyfriend so deeply hidden that I had no idea I was going out with his father. And he only just found out that I work for the newspaper. But don't be too worried. Although I love Qi Canxi and he loves Lin Lin and me, and wants us all to be a family, at the moment it all seems very difficult. Dr Lin knows I have a new partner and is now refusing to grant me a divorce. He comes round here three times a week now, and seeing that Lin Lin isn't leaving the house, he takes the boy out to the cinema. It's true, if I were to marry Qi Cangxi and you're with Qi Deming, it would make things slightly awkward. I couldn't exactly be your mother-in-law, could I? Would you have to call me mother, or just Nana like before?' Huang Weina laughed loudly, and her hand shook, spilling the ash from her cigarette onto her silver silk nightdress.

'Qi Cangxi must be at least twenty years older than you. How can you want to marry a man that old?' I asked.

'I understand, you want to marry Qi Deming,' Huang Weina said, pulling a face.

'It's been a long time since we've been in touch,' I said.

'But that doesn't mean that you don't still love each other,' Huang Weina said.

By the time I left Huang Weina's house, the sky was already getting dark. I went to the typhoon shelter and had a bowl of crabmeat and tofu, and drank half a bottle of white wine, before making my way back home in a drunken stupor. When I got to the door and pulled out my key, I noticed my checked umbrella, the one I had left in the print factory, propped up by the door, and stuck on the door was a note in Qi Deming's handwriting that read: *Not carrying an umbrella on a rainy day, isn't that just asking for trouble? I've never met a girl as forgetful as you, losing stuff left, right and centre.*

The returned umbrella gave me the courage to ring Qi Deming. I went inside, put down the umbrella and dialled his number straight away.

'Thank you for returning my umbrella!'

'Congratulations on inheriting a house!' Qi Deming said. 'Now you are a rich little homeowner, you don't have to worry about getting married!'

'Stop blabbing,' I said. 'Do you know about the relationship between Huang Weina and your dad?'

'Yep,' said Qi Deming. 'Look, my dad has been single for so many years and he's messed around with lots of women in that time, but this is the first time he's been serious about someone. If he wants to marry Huang Weina, I'll be dutiful about it and not stand in their way. I guess that means things are over between us. I can't imagine you'll accept your best friend as your mother-in-law?'

'Who says I want to marry you?' I said.

'Hey, wealth changes people!' Qi Deming replied. 'It was just a stab in the dark.'

'Why didn't you wait around when you brought back the umbrella?' I asked.

'I had to rush to the airport. I need to go to Sichuan for a few days. I'll come and see you when I get back. You can host me at your luxury mansion, cook me something European to go with the style of the house!'

'You're demanding European food now, are you? You'd be lucky if you got a bowl of egg noodles! You haven't forgotten your suitcase, have you?' I asked with a giggle.

Qi Deming gave a mischievous chuckle and said, 'Comrade Zhao Xiao'e, which of the two items in the case are you asking about?'

'Bastard!' I said.

'I've just arrived at the airport. I'll see you on my return.' Qi Deming hung up the phone.

Five days later, Qi Deming returned. As his airplane landed at Harbin Taiping International Airport, I was out on the balcony watching the gleaming red sun setting in the sky. He sent a text to tell me he'd arrived safely and asked how my European food preparations were going. *A luxury homeowner and a pot of beef and persimmon soup are awaiting you,* I replied.

Qi Deming never got to taste my soup. Moments after sending me that text he started to walk down the gangway, where he suffered a sudden myocardial infarction and fell down head first, never to get back up. His suitcase arrived at the arrival hall conveyor belt along with all the other suitcases and was slowly rotated round. After all the other suitcases had been claimed, it was just his suitcase left, like a lone goose from a flock of wild geese, standing all alone on the dark conveyor-belt.

The person who had given me both nightmares and joy departed, just like that. I didn't go to his funeral; Qi Deming didn't like it when girls cried and if I were to attend there was no way I would remain dry-eyed. I just gave his father a call and told him that Qi Deming had a shroud in his suitcase, and he should be wearing it when cremated.

After Qi Deming's death, the world started to feel like a very dark place. Walking along a straight road gave me the sensation of trekking through mud and made me feel overwhelmingly heavy. I didn't eat for three days nor did I feel any hunger. On cool nights my body felt boiling hot, and in the afternoon when the sun was fierce, I felt so cold I shivered. I continued to experience that white space inside my head and was unable to sleep at night.

I kept forgetting things; the only thing fixed deeply in my mind was something that Qi Deming had said, about how if he ever proposed to me, he would do so in the old synagogue. One day I wore a black skirt with the red flower patterns, the one I'd bought with my biological father's money, and with it, a small black suit jacket. I inserted a red rose into the top pocket of the suit jacket at an angle and set off there all alone.

The synagogue was like a country manor. It had a musty old smell and a sense of rustic goodwill. There was a girl on the reception desk with her hair in a ponytail. I told her I'd come to see one of their guests, we'd arranged it on the phone and he'd be coming down soon. Not the slightest bit suspicious of my story, she told me to go round the corner to the small ground floor lounge where I was welcome to sit and wait.

That lounge was long and narrow, shaped like a banana, and it was simple and cosy. A vast array of old photographs hung on its mottled walls, while cylindrical sheepskin lamps in the hallway cast down a pale yellow light. I picked a small square table for two people to sit opposite each other and sat there gently stroking the table's blue and white checked tablecloth. Addressing the chair opposite me I said, 'Qi Deming, if you still want to be my husband, then please propose to me!' The chair opposite was empty, no one there to say anything in response; the only sound came from the old sofa next to it, where one of the two cats, one ginger and one black, snuggled up sweetly together, let out a gentle sigh. That was it. I lost control and started screaming hysterically.

That was the moment I went crazy. Losing your mind is as easy as that.

By the time I was released from the mental asylum, it was already the New Year. I had no idea how autumn had managed to come and go from the city, and winter to return. I didn't want to see anyone, not even relatives or friends and I didn't want to know any of their news. The asylum doctor paid me a visit once a week and advised me to write down everything I had been through, saying this would help to move me a step closer towards recovery.

Living in the house left to me by Ji Lianna, accompanied by the cold current sweeping through the city, watching the evening frost form on the window, I picked up my pen and started to recall. I was no longer a proofreader. It was the first time I had experienced the beauty of words, words that were neither right or wrong. As soon as I was able to order my memories, my mental health would return to normal, according to my doctor. But I was afraid of normal, because it meant my suffering could return. I wished that I could turn myself into a bird perched upon Ji Lianna's wall clock, to be with the dying time. I didn't want to hear the sound of time, because time was now a dried up river to me and it had lost all meaning.

In this avant-garde novella, a writer named Ge Fei retreats to the
beautiful solitude of the Waterside to finish his novel, which is inspired
by the Revelations of St. John. He perceives ominous and portentous
signs in the natural landscape around him, particularly in a flock of
brown birds that flies periodically past his window. The arrival of a mys-
terious woman named Qi magnifies his anxiety and sense of temporal
disorientation, calling into question his grasp on reality.

Ge Fei is one of China's foremost writers of experimental fiction
and currently serves as Professor of Literature at Tsinghua University
in Beijing. Frequently referred to as the 'Chinese Borges', he is the
winner of the 2014 Lu Xun Literary Prize for fiction and the 2015
Mao Dun Literary Prize.

Petulia's Rouge Tin

Su Tong

China, early 1950s: Two friends find themselves on their way to a re-education camp for those not adhering to the standards of the new order. Who would have anticipated that Petulia, stripped of her silk gowns, would be forced to denounce the Red Delight Pavilion? Or believed that Autumn Grace would cry in desperation as nuns shave off her locks? After years working side-by-side, the scent of rouge filling their memories keeps them close, despite the struggles life throws at them. Until one day, the promise of love becomes a temptation neither can deny …

Su Tong was born in Suzhou, China. He is the author of numerous novels, including *Raise the Red Lantern*, which was adapted into the award-winning film by Zhang Yimou. Su Tong has also been awarded the prestigious 2015 Mao Dun Literary Prize and 2009 Man Asian Literary Prize, and was shortlisted for the Man Booker International Prize.